LINC

THORNE BROTHER SERIES

AMBER ALLEE

For everyone who has ever fallen hard
and fast with their person.

LINC

CHAPTER ONE

Linc

"The jury finds the defendant not guilty," the foreman reads the verdict from the official document. The courtroom erupts in cheers as Judge Smith bangs his gavel to regain control of the room.

I can't help the smirk on my face as I pat my client on the shoulder in congratulations. His case has taken me a year to get to this victory and it wasn't an easy one.

As one of the top attorneys in the country I pride myself in having a winning record. I've made a name for myself over the years and am sought after by everyone. My clients range from celebrities to CEOs to anyone else who can pay my exuberant hourly fee.

"Better luck next time, Buttons," I say to the district attorney, Burt Buttons, after the judge has left the courtroom and we're all gathering our materials up.

"You know what, Linc? I hope you and your brother are proud and sleep well every night after defending some of the worst people to walk our streets," he sneers.

"I'm just doing my job," I respond. "If you'd do a better job at bringing evidence then maybe you'd win one occasionally."

His face flushes red and I can see his frustration seeping out.

"You know as well as I do that your client was guilty and deserves to be behind bars." He takes a step towards me.

"Even if I thought that was the case, which I don't, every person has the right to counsel and a fair trial," I tell him, matching a step toward him.

Burt Buttons and I went to law school the same time at Yale. We didn't run in the same circles but he was always trying to outshine me for some reason. Burt thought he was the smartest person in every room he entered and I took great pleasure knocking him down a peg or two throughout those years.

I lost to him for the very first time right after I started my own firm. The next day, he took out an entire page in the paper boasting about it, trying to make me look like a fool. That was five years ago, and the last time he ever won against me or my firm.

"What is that now, Burt, fifty-eight to one?" I brag because I can't stand this bastard. I can't prove it but I'm sure he has falsified some evidence to try to win a few cases against me over the last five years. I might take on some rough clients but like I said, everyone deserves to have the right to a fair trial and counsel.

His eyes narrow, "One of these days I'm going to best you, or that snot nosed brother of yours, in the worst way and there will be nothing you'll be able to do about it."

"I look forward to it," I challenge. What I really want to do is knock his teeth in for even mentioning my baby brother Levi. If there is one thing in this world I protect at all costs it's him and has been since we were little.

He turns on his cheap loafers and storms out the swinging wooden partition that separates us from the gallery.

"How long do you think the DA's office will continue to keep him with his losing record?" I hear Olivia, one of my partners at the firm, ask.

I turn as she holds out my briefcase for me to take. "For his sake and my ego I hope they never get rid of him."

"Well, you sure stuck it to him," Kevin Jenkins pipes up with a big smile on his face.

Kevin has been part of the firm for almost a year. He's been a real go-getter since joining. The last few months, he's taken on more and more cases as he shows us how capable and smart he is. His win record is higher than most of the office. It's impressive for someone who just came not long ago.

"The guy was a prick back in law school and hasn't changed at all since then," I say.

"I'd love to try my hand with him," Kevin boasts, still reeling from the win of our case. He's pretty cocky, like most new guys, and I think it gives him the edge our firm has.

"Linc refuses to let anyone ride solo against Burt. I think he's made it his personal mission to always be the lead chair with cases against him," Olivia states as she checks her phone.

"Damn right I do," I say.

"PR just sent over the talking points for the media circus outside."

I pull out my phone and see the message. Looking over the email I make a mental note on which ones I want to speak on. I'm riding on the winning train when I decide to let Kevin have a small piece of the attention. He was the one who did all the grunt and leg work helping with this case.

"After I finish speaking on the talking points, why don't you answer some of the reporter's questions," I offer to the young associate. I watch Olivia raise an eyebrow, shocked I'd let someone else take over the spotlight on such a big case.

"Really?" he looks like I've just handed him a million dollars. "That'd be great."

"Don't make me regret this," I tell him, then check my watch.

After I make sure the team has everything, we walk out into the hallway. The media is expecting a news conference that we've already prepped for and will be making shortly. Our client has already been ushered out through the backdoor and is on his way out of the country for a while until the news dies down.

In the hall, we start to make our way toward the front of the building, when I catch sight of the most beautiful woman I've ever seen turn the corner. She's holding a piece of paper in one hand while looking around at the different doors and signs. My feet physically stop and I feel someone bump into me from behind. It's like the world took a pause when our eyes connect. Something in my stomach twists and a tingling shiver crawls across my arms and shoulders. Her chocolate brown hair lays in soft curls below her shoulders as her hazel eyes take me in. She has the perfect bow shaped mouth and the cutest button nose.

"Lincoln, are you okay?" I'm being asked but I don't dare take my eyes off the angel in front of me, for fear she might disappear.

A light pink blush caresses her cheeks and she turns her eyes from mine. Well, that won't do.

I walk around the team in front of me and stride over to the woman who physically takes my breath away. In the distance, I vaguely hear my name being called.

"Do you need some help, angel?" I hear myself ask.

I watch as she stares up at my lips and I can't help but smile down at her. She's even more gorgeous up close. I lightly place my hand on her upper arm and we both jolt from our skin touching.

A small gasp leaves her glossy lips from the contact. Her skin is like silk on my fingertips, making me want to stroke every part of her delicious body.

She shakes her head slightly, "I'm looking for room," she looks down at the paper in her hand and then back up to my eyes. "208."

"It's up the stairs and down the hall on your left," I tell her, knowing this building like the back of my hand. "What are you here for?"

"I got a parking ticket," her voice comes out low at first but then a little louder at the end. She takes her free hand and tucks some of her hair behind her ear.

"I can walk you over there and show you, if you want," I offer then sweep my hand toward the stairs that lead up to the next floor. "Can I see your ticket?"

"Are you sure? Your group looks to be waiting on you," she says then nods to over my shoulder.

"They can wait," I say, not even bothering to glance their way, then place my hand on the small of her back, guiding her to the steps. She hands over the paper and I quickly scan the form. Everly Bryant. What a beautiful name.

"Do you work here?" she asks as we ascend the stairs. I catch her out of the corner of my eye checking me out.

"I'm an attorney," I say and pass her back the paper.

"Ohh," she comments but the way she says it makes me think I've said the wrong thing. We stop at the top step and I watch her give me a once over. I know I'm a good-looking fucker and have been gawked at most of my life, but seeing her look me over makes me start to think she might not like what she sees. Not once in my life, have I ever had to question myself in the way I look. I'm quite a cocky bastard but this woman might just give me a complex and makes me question everything I thought about myself.

Raising an eyebrow in question, she shakes her head, as if ridding something from her thoughts.

"You don't like attorneys?" My mind races as my heart drops to the bottom of my stomach.

"No, no not at all, I just didn't… I guess I can see it now," she mentions as if talking to herself.

"See what?"

She smiles. "The confidence, or arrogance."

"Wow, way to box me into the stigma of attorneys." I try to sound wounded, making her laugh.

"Am I wrong?" She crosses her arms and raises an eyebrow, challenging me, and I'm here for her playfulness.

"You got me there." My phone buzzes, and I reluctantly reach in my pocket to retrieve it. Being an attorney, and the boss, means I'm on duty twenty-four seven in case a client is sitting down at the police station after doing some dumb shit that put them there.

"What's your name, angel?" I ask as we head down the hall and almost to the door she needs. I already know it, so I'm pushing to get more personal.

She places her hand on her forehead and rolls her eyes, "I can't believe how rude I am. I'm Everly, sorry," she says and holds her hand out for me to shake. "I'm usually not like this, you must think I'm scatterbrained."

"Definitely not. You're just so enamored by me that I took your thoughts and breath away," I joke, encasing her soft hand in mine.

She giggles and its music to my ears.

"What are you doing later tonight?"

"You haven't given me your name yet," she sasses. "I've been schooled to never tell anything personal to strangers, especially the attorney types." She slides her hand out of mine and my hand itches to latch it back and never let it go.

"You were raised right then, Everly. I'm Lincoln Thorne." I reach into my jacket pocket and hand her my business card.

She puts her hand out to take the card and I make sure to brush my fingers against hers, feeling that buzz again when our skin touches.

"Thank you, Lincoln, for helping me find the right office," she says as she places my card in her back pocket. "And I'm meeting with some friends at a bar tonight if you'd like to come hang out."

"If you're there then count me in." She tells me the name of the bar and time she'll be there just as my phone vibrates again. "Can I get your number and call you later?"

She shakes her head, "If you show up tonight then I might give it to you. I can't be giving out my digits to strangers or possible criminals."

That makes me chuckle.

"Angel, the only law breaker between us is the one who's here to settle a ticket," I say then lean in and give her a soft peck on her cheek. She smells like vanilla. "See you tonight, Everly."

I turn and walk back down the hall. When I'm almost to the stairs, I stop and turn back.

"Do you want me to get you out of that ticket?" I call out right before she's about to enter the room to 208.

Everly stops and looks up at me, "No, I did it so I need to pay the price," she admits. "Maybe next time." She laughs, then waves at me before she walks through the entryway and is out of sight.

I wait a few beats before descending the stairs, not looking back for fear I'd never leave her side if I didn't get out of there soon. When I reach the bottom of the steps, I see my team still waiting on me.

"Everything okay?" Olivia asks as she approaches me with the oddest look on her face.

"Everything is perfect. Why?"

Olivia shakes her head, "You have the biggest smile on your face, and you were whistling." Was I? "Who was that?"

I'm sure I've caught her off guard with my actions. I've never let anything interfere with clients or business before, so I'm sure I've thrown her for a loop.

I look back up toward the second floor where Everly is and can't stop the smile from forming on my lips. My aunt always said growing up, "If you want something bad enough then say it into existence." So, with every part of my being, I give it a try for the first time.

"That, my friend, was my future wife."

CHAPTER TWO

"Mr. Thorne, I'm heading out for the evening. Is there anything I can get you before I go?" Ruby, my ever-efficient secretary, asks. She's been with me from the beginning and was my first hire after Olivia, my business partner, when I started Thorne Law Firm. She is fifty-eight and has three grandkids who she gushes about on the daily. Her desk is littered with photos and finger paintings.

"No, that will be all, Ruby. Have a great weekend and kiss those grandbabies," I say as I press the button on the phone to respond.

The thought of babies makes me cringe slightly. I've never thought of myself having kids with the lifestyle that I've grown accustomed to. My life consists of work, sex, more work and buying the latest toy for my car collection, or something else to get my adrenaline pumping.

"You too, Mr. Thorne. Don't forget you're meeting Mr. Levi and Reid for drinks in thirty minutes."

"Got it," I answer, not letting her know that I'm really meeting up with a woman I met just hours earlier. Levi, my brother, is tagging along after chatting with him on my way from the courthouse earlier back to my office. I'd told him I'd met his future sister-in-law and that I was meeting up with her later this evening. Him being the nosy prick that he is, decided to meet me there as well, to see the woman who brought me to my bachelor knees—his words not mine. He also called our cousin, who we think of as our brother, Reid, and shared the news to him.

She says her goodbye and my office goes silent once again. Shutting down my computer, I gather up my case files and lock them away for tomorrow. I've got no plans this weekend so working on a Saturday and Sunday is nothing new for me. I've got a huge case next and can't afford to get behind. My client has been accused of murdering two people and I think I've got just what I need to get him off and have the entire case thrown out of court.

The elevator dings and I step out into the garage that hosts my Limited-Edition Bugatti. She is my favorite baby and I only get her out on Fridays, when I know I'm going out on the town. Being photographed and my face splashed across every outlet on a weekly basis is part of being a high-powered attorney, so making sure to arrive in style is something that is expected of me.

Los Angeles traffic is absolutely horrendous, so when we hang out, I make sure Levi and Reid always pick a place close to where we live. We usually avoid the crowd on Friday nights, but I've got a date with an angel, and I'd meet her anywhere she wanted.

One thing I love about LA is that just about every place has valet parking. Tossing my keys to the guy, I slip him a hundred dollars, telling him to make sure she stays in the same shape as I'm leaving her, and to keep her parked in front of the bar for an easy getaway when we're done here.

"Lincoln!" I hear my name being yelled as I walk in and see

both Levi and Reid sitting on a stool in the middle of the bar. They are already halfway through their pints of beer as I approach my brothers.

"Hey bro." We greet each other the same way we've always done, a hard man hug.

One thing I always love about Reid is that he is never jealous of me or Levi for coming into his family and stealing some of the attention of his parents. He welcomed us with open arms and never thought of us as anything other than his brother. Of course, we fight like cats and dogs, but at the end of the day, we know he is our best friend.

"I see you couldn't wait for the evening to start." I nod towards their almost empty glasses.

"Well, I never know if you'll be held up with a case or not." Levi shrugs and waves down the bartender. "Plus I wanted to get here early so that we could talk more about this woman you think you are going to marry."

"Not a lot to tell but that she's perfect," I say. "Came out of the courtroom after scoring another big win off of Button's and there she was."

"Just like that," Levi scoffs.

"The light filtered through the window above us and it looked as though she was an angel standing there with a halo around her head. Stopped me straight in my tracks." The bartender pours my draft beer in a mug then slides it over the countertop. After taking a gulp I set it down and say, "Felt like my life was never going to be the same."

"Now that is going to make Grandma happy to hear," Reid says, then waves for another drink.

Thirty minutes later, the game showing on the wall behind the bar is halfway over and the crowd has finally calmed down for halftime. I still have another twenty minutes before Everly is supposed to be here but I'm anxious that she might stand me up. The door chimes and I happen to look over as Levi is telling me the latest real estate property he's looking to purchase while Reid is talking sports with the guy next to him.

Have you ever had a moment in your life where your life starts a reel like in the movies? You can just picture everything in the order it's going to happen. You stop breathing as if you're suspended in midair waiting for the clock to be reset. This is that moment for me. *Again.*

She mesmerizes me and something about her draws me in. It's like she has this aura around her, letting everyone in the bar know she is something special. My breath stalls in those few seconds as I watch her giggle at something her friend is saying.

Hook.

Line.

Sinker.

Even her giggle sets me on a dreamy path. It's like seeing her for the first time.

She is wearing a white mini dress that fits her like a glove with tall heels. Even from here I can tell she was a shorty with those skyscraper shoes on. She stands at most five-two against my six-two easily but those legs look like they go on for days. Her chest is heavy and just barely showing the tops of her perfectly perky tits that fill out the top of the dress. She has the fullest pink lips that I'd like to bite between my teeth. When she wets her lips with her bubblegum tongue, I know I'm a goner. Her smile lights up the entire bar and her hazel eyes shine brightly against her chocolate-colored hair.

Reid snaps his fingers in my face, bringing me out of my trance. I know that she is something special and I'll be damned if she is going to leave here with some asshole; other than me, of course. I'll find a way to make her mine. During the day, I'm built to negotiate and persuade people to see things my way and she'll be no different. No, I saw her first this afternoon and there isn't any other outcome that is going to be acceptable. I am Lincoln Thorne, the wealthiest attorney in the city, and I run this town. So, what does a good looking thirty-four-year-old guy who has the world at his fingertips do? I leave my brothers in the dust and make my way over to where she and her friends are all congregating. Normally, I have a contingency plan in place for every occasion. I am a scheduled person, structure is my life, but this little slip of a woman set my mapped-out life up in flames. All it took was one look into her bright hazel eyes and I knew she was mine. The look she gave me when we were almost nose to nose tells me that she is just as captivated as me. That what we were feeling at the courthouse wasn't a one-time thing.

"You have plans for the next sixty-five years?" The words are spilling out of me before I can stop them. I am never one to seek out women, they always find and pursue me.

"She isn't interested buddy," her friend, who she came in with, spouts waving me away, but I ignore her and keep my eyes focused on my future wife.

"I think I might," she wiggles her eyebrows and I can tell her heart rate is racing from the pulsing vein in her neck. I am good at reading people for a living and she is going to be all mine.

"What's your name, angel?" I ask even though we already know each other.

"Everly," she says, playing along.

"Well, Everly, I'm Lincoln Thorne."

"I'm glad you came," she says, stepping closer to me as the

crowded bar around us gets louder. "I didn't really think you'd show up."

"Let's go across the street to the quiet coffee bar and get a drink. Then we can discuss how our future together is going to pan out."

And it's that simple. She tells her friends bye, much to the protest of her group of friends, and I guide her out of the bar and across the street to a small coffee shop, leaving behind all the noise. We order at the counter and I stand back and watch how she greets and speaks with each person she comes in contact with. Her smile never falters as she engages with the employees.

"So, Everly, where have you been all my life?"

"Do all those lines really work on women?" she asks as our coffee is delivered to the little half circular booth in the corner. We're so close our thighs are touching.

"Not sure. You're the first one I've ever said that to." She rolls her eyes and I can't help but chuckle. "Really, it's true. I've never used a line on a woman before now."

"Well, then you might need a little more practice, Casanova."

We both sip our hot coffee a bit and I can't help but enjoy her presence. She brings a bit of fresh air and is like no other woman I've had contact with, and I've had a lot of women in my presence.

"So, when you're not out with your friends, what occupies your time?"

"I'm a massage therapist at a spa here in town."

Automatically, I reach out for her hands and caress them. She's the smallest, most delicate thing ever and her hands are no different. Without thinking, I'm pressing them to my lips and can't help the smallest moan when the petal soft skin touches me. The thought of her touching every inch of my body ignites a fire inside of me.

"What spa?" I ask. I'd love nothing more than to throw her tiny frame over my shoulder and head to my penthouse. Kidnapping is a serious offense, but I'm willing to try and argue in a court of law, if it'd get me time alone with her.

"It's off of Hollywood Boulevard… called Allure Spa and Wellness." I file that information away and focus back. She still hasn't asked for her hand back so I take it as a good sign and continue to hold her close. How have I never thought about getting a massage before? God, I could've met her long before now. Looking at her she seems young, college age maybe.

"How long have you been there?" Jesus, that's all I need is to be hitting on a woman who's barely legal. She was in the bar so I take it as she's old enough but she looks so damn young with her small petite size.

"Three years." She gives me a knowing look. "I'm twenty-three by the way," she offers, like she can read my mind. If she only knew what I wish we were really doing rather than drinking coffee, I'd have her blushing the same shade as her kissable lips.

"That's good to know. Did you grow up here in LA or are you a transplant?"

"Grew up north of Sacramento. After high school, college didn't interest me so I looked into other avenues and found massage therapy. Went to school for nine months and here I am. My best friend, Saylor, she's the one I came with tonight, her family owns Allure and multiple chains throughout the U.S. I started working for their company. She owns a bakery not far from here."

"Can I get you guys a refill?" The barista asks, interrupting us as he makes his way around the shop. I don't miss the ogling as he appraises Everly. I shift so that I'm practically towering over her small frame while giving him the fuck off look. His eyes widen when he finally looks over at my death stare hopefully realizing that he doesn't have a shot in hell with my girl.

We both decline getting back into our little quiet bubble once again.

"So, what do you do for fun when you're not picking women up at bars?"

I have to laugh at her question. I can tell she doesn't believe that I don't do this often. I don't because in LA women are served on a silver platter to rich, famous men such as myself.

"I work a lot so that takes up most of my time but when I get some free time my brothers, Levi and Reid, and I like to do any outdoor activities. We like skydiving, hiking, surfing and skiing. Reid and I both got our pilot's license two years ago."

"Wow, that's really impressive. I love being outdoors too. Your other brother didn't want to join in on being a pilot?"

"Levi thought it was a waste of money. He prefers to buy real estate, fix it up then sell for a profit when he isn't in the courtroom."

"Oh, so your brothers are attorneys also?"

"Just Levi. Reid is a dentist."

"Wow, two attorneys and a dentist. I bet your parents are really proud," she says sincerely. If she only knew that Levi and I were actually raised by my aunt and uncle after our parents OD'd on some bad heroin. But there's no reason to bring up bad memories tonight, so I go the easy route.

"They are. My dad is also an attorney and Mom is a paralegal at his office."

My phone buzzes and I've never hated the device more knowing that the message might take me away from Everly right now. Thankfully it's Reid wondering if he should wait at the bar or leave since the game's been over for hours and the bar is getting ready to close. Levi apparently met a woman and left a few hours ago.

Checking my watch, I can see that it's almost two in the morning. *How did time get away from us?* I send a quick response for him not to wait and that I'll call him tomorrow.

Everly has her phone out texting when I pocket mine.

"Everything alright?" I ask when she places her phone face down on the table.

"Yeah, Saylor just wants to make sure that I'm still alive." She smiles and that simple motion does things to me.

"I hope you told her that you're in good hands." I reach back over, taking her hand back in mine.

"I did. I told her you were an attorney." We both bust out with laughter and I can't help but feel like this is how it's supposed to be. Is this the feeling of finding the one person in the world that finishes off the last piece of the puzzle in your life? She'd probably file a restraining order first thing Monday morning if she could read my mind at the thoughts I'm having after only knowing her for such a short amount of time.

"What are your plans for the weekend?" I ask when I see that we're the last ones in the coffee shop. Off in the corner, the barista waves then points to his watch letting me know we need to get the hell out of there.

"I work half day tomorrow, well today, then I'm off until Tuesday."

"I'd like to spend the weekend with you."

"Weekend?" I know I shock her from the way her voice squeaks, but why wait? If she lets me, I'd already have her back at my place naked in my bed. "Isn't there like a few days in between before we see each other again?"

She obviously doesn't date confident men who know what they want.

"Let's cut to the chase so we can begin our lives together."

"You sound like this is a done deal, like there aren't any other options." She gives a nervous laugh.

"I'm not a man who likes to waste time. I like results when I see something I want. When I saw you this afternoon and then again tonight, I knew we'd be perfect for each other."

"Wow, okay um…" She brings her hand up to her forehead and starts to rub it close to her hairline. It's a nervous tick she has and a dead giveaway that she needs more reassurance.

Being an attorney, you have to be able to read the people you select to be on a jury if you have any chance at winning. Watching a person and figuring them out has taken me years to learn and perfect but my team and I are really good at reading people and their signals.

"Give me your number and I'll call you later on today," I say and pick up her phone from the table.

"Are you always so bossy or is that an attorney thing?" She teases and I think we're going to fit together like perfect puzzle pieces.

"It's a *me* thing," I answer and plug my number into her phone then send myself a text.

I drop some cash on the table and reach for her hand to help her out of the booth. A tingle flushes up my wrist as I lead her out and onto the sidewalk.

"Did you drive?" I ask as we cross the street.

"No, I rode with Saylor. I can grab an Uber or cab," she says then starts to look up and down the street.

"Not a chance in hell," I tell her. This will also give me a chance to see where she lives and not have to use the firm's PI to get me the information.

Tugging her back in front of the bar across the street, I hand the valet my ticket as we wait on the curb for them to bring my car over to us.

"There's someone following us," Everly leans in whispering close to my ear, as the smell of vanilla invades my nose. I have to catch myself to not sniff too loudly as to alert her.

I follow her line of sight and see who she's talking about.

Dale.

Now this is going to be interesting to explain.

"It's his job to follow," I say and she tears her eyes away from Dale to me. She looks utterly confused and it makes me chuckle. "He's with me. Handling high profile cases sometimes means that I'm not the most liked person in America."

"Oh." Not only is she a smart woman but a very observant one at that. At least she's aware of her surroundings.

"It's just a precaution, nothing to worry about." I wave it off, hoping she's not too uncomfortable having someone follow us around, but I can't take the chance that a psycho family member doesn't come out of the woodwork to attack me for doing my job. She nods and I can tell she wants to ask more, but thankfully the valet rolls up with my car.

"This is your car?!?" Everly's shocked tone makes me glad I picked the Bugatti tonight.

"She's a beauty, isn't she?"

I hold the door and assist her in the car, almost catching a glimpse of her upper thigh. A groan leaves me as I close the door, thinking about what she has on under that white dress of hers.

The drive over to her apartment is a quiet one. I'm not sure what to think as she seems to have built walls all around her. I want to reach over and snatch her hand but I'm not sure that's the right move.

All too soon we pull up to her apartment complex but neither of us make a move. Finally, after several long moments, Everly shifts her tiny body towards me.

"I had a nice time tonight Lincoln. Thank you for the coffee and chat."

Why does she sound like this is the last time we're ever going to see each other again? Surely, I didn't blow it that bad. We were just talking about making weekend plans, so what changed?

She moves to find the handle to the door but I stop her with my hand on her exposed thigh.

"What just happened? I thought we both had a great night?" I question.

"We did, I did."

"Then what is it? Why do you sound like you're about to block me from your phone?" Not like that would stop me from getting in contact with her.

She takes a breath, like she's steeling herself for something.

"We… we just come from two totally different walks of life, Linc." She starts and I notice how she calls me Linc instead of my full name that I prefer, except when it comes out of her mouth. "I mean, you seem to live the fast life and have guards and drive a car worth millions of dollars. I'm a massage therapist who makes her living through tips and has credit card debt and gets parking tickets. I'm not the type of girl who's into one night stands or wants to be with someone because they are famous. I'm pretty simple and basic."

I tuck a stray hair behind her ear then place a finger under her chin.

"You are anything but basic or simple. I find you to be the most exquisite woman to ever grace my life. All of this," I motion around. "It's nothing to worry about. The moment I saw you I knew I had to talk to you and be in your presence. I don't care what your background is or if you only eat grilled cheese for all three meals. Don't say no to something before we've even had a chance to become forever."

I can tell she's thinking things over and warring with herself. Never in my life have I had to convince a woman to be with me. It's a humbling experience to say the least.

"Just give it a chance, Everly." I squeeze her hand then bring it up to my lips. "I promise you won't regret it."

There's a glint in her eyes and I know I've won. A small smile twitches on her pink lips and she nods. Not being able to hold off any longer, I lean over the console and capture her lips to mine. She tastes like candy and her lips are as soft as I imagined they would be. Taking one hand, I glide it up to the back of her head at the nape. She lets out a soft moan opening her mouth ever so slightly. I take that moment to slip my tongue in to explore hers. I've never been one that enjoys kissing but the more I kiss Everly the more I'm addicted to her lips.

Just when my dick starts to rip through my suit pants and attack her, I pull back and rest my forehead to hers. My eyes slide downward and I watch as her chest heaves to catch her breath. The teenage boy in me cops a look at the best-looking rack I've ever seen. Everly is doing things to me and making me feel things that I only hear others speak about.

"I'll call you later today," I say looking into her bright hazel eyes.

She nods, biting her bottom lip and it makes me want to jam the car in gear and take her back to my place and never let her go. But I can't. I need to show her that I'm the one who's not in her league; I'm not worthy of her but I want to be.

I climb out the car and make my way around to her side. Everly is wobbly getting out of the car as we walk up the concrete path to enter her apartment building. I bite the inside of my cheek as I watch her hips sway left then right as she makes her way inside.

"Goodnight, baby!" I call after her right before the door closes.

I can hear her giggle then say it back.

Man, I'm in trouble. The good kind for once.

CHAPTER THREE

Waking the next morning, I slam my hand down on my alarm clock to stop the alarm blaring. Ugh! Didn't I just go to bed? My tired eyes finally focus and see that it's eight fifteen. Why did I have to wake up? I was having the dream of a lifetime about meeting a guy and making out in a car. Wait…

Quickly sitting straight up in bed, I look around the room. It DID happen. A smile graces my exhausted face, thinking about how last night played out.

Lincoln.

My second alarm goes off, this time from my phone, alerting me to get my butt moving or I'll be late. Begrudgingly, I slip out from the warm comfort of my bed and into the small bathroom of my one-bedroom apartment. The pricing in LA for a place to live is outrageous but to be in a safe area you have to pay for safety. It's not much but it's been mine to call home for the last three years.

Saylor, my best friend, lives down the hall in a spacious two-bedroom apartment. Her grandparents were planning to buy her a new home in a gated community up in the hills but she's been protesting against it. She doesn't want to be that far away from the clubs, bar and action, as she puts it. Saylor thinks this is our time to shine, be young and free and to sow our wild oats. She also doesn't work at the spa but owns her own bakery. She's been open for almost a year and has had such great success so far. She's truly gifted in creating sweet treats that everyone drools over.

We've been best friends since I was ten and she was twelve years old. Our dads were in the Navy together and we lived next door to each other on base. Our friendship was instant from the start and she would always defend me against the older bullies. We tried living together at the beginning but I quickly learned that I needed my own space. Saylor can be on the messy side, after always having had someone to come and clean up after her. Me on the other hand, I've always tried to keep myself and living quarters tidy and manageable.

Hopping into the shower, I let the hot water wake my lazy body to be able to function for my half day of work. The thought of Lincoln calling me later has me hurrying through my routine so that my day can start then be over quickly. Once shaved to perfection, I go in search of my work uniform, which usually consists of a tight, thin white blouse along with tight black dress pants that hug you snuggly across every inch of your body. On weekends, like today, we are to wear a pair of tight short black hot pants with black killer heels. It shows off more skin than I prefer but the tips from the men are a nice balance, I guess.

I give myself one last look in the mirror by the door, making sure my hair has the right amount of bounce and curl. Heading down the elevator, I can't help but check my phone to make sure I've got enough battery life to last me throughout the day.

Don't get your hopes up Everly, he might not call. My cynical self rears its ugly head.

Allure Spa and Wellness is a large two-story modern building in the premiere area of Hollywood Boulevard. Everyone who's anyone comes here to get pampered. Our clientele list hosts an array of people through all the upper-class socialites from actors, directors to musicians, songwriters to bankers, businessmen and so forth. Our prices are amongst the most expensive but people come from all over just to say they've had treatments here.

"Hey girl," Lisa, our receptionist, greets after I place all my things in my locker in the staff quarters.

"Good morning Lisa, how was your evening?"

"Wonderful, as usual. Frankie and I curled up on the sofa and watched a thriller movie." She beams when talking about her cat. Everyone here calls her the cat lady but I think she's just been tainted by too many bad relationships.

"That's great. How's the schedule look today?" I ask, coming around the desk to print out my day so that I can keep a copy with me.

"Well," She pauses for a moment then gasps. "It looks like all four of your clients have been reassigned."

"What!" I hiss in the quiet lobby.

"It shows that someone moved your people and you've got one person who's going to fill up those four hours."

I practically shove her out of the way to get a better look at the screen. I might be little but I can pack a punch when necessary.

"I don't understand? Why would anyone want a four-hour massage?"

"Could be an athlete that has a lot of tension needing to be worked out." Lisa shrugs and checks in a guest, who's waiting to be signed in. "You better hurry, they checked in ten minutes ago. It says they specifically asked for you." She playfully shoves me back out of the way and begins typing on the computer.

Great. Just great. I usually get a break in between clients but this person is going to give my hands and fingers cramps if I'm working on them the entire time.

My room is number nine down the long hallway of the treatment rooms. Our clients each have their own individual rooms with a locker, which is basically a waiting room until we're ready for them to come in. The treatment room is colored in calming dark gray-blue colors. I've got a water feature in the corner, with lit vanilla candles, and soft cords of music playing over the speakers.

Once I make sure everything is in order with the sheets and my lotion, I knock on the waiting room door for my client to come through. The door opens and I'm shocked to see who's standing on the other side, in a white robe and flip flops.

"Lincoln? What…what are you doing here?" I can't believe he's here, standing in front of me.

"I asked for a demonstration last night, remember?" he says like we had this planned from the start.

"Yes, but I didn't think you'd get an appointment right away. You do know that by blocking off four hours, you're going to be paying thousands of dollars, right?" I inform him. "I could've done this for free at my place if you'd have waited."

"But then I wouldn't get to see you in your element."

"This is crazy," I mumble. "Come lie down, let's get you started."

I walk over to the cabinet and grab a bottle of my favorite lotion. We have different types of oils and lotions depending on what the client likes; some have allergies so we have to have a variety that caters to all.

"Should I be on my stomach or back?" Lincoln asks as I'm still facing away from him.

Turning with the bottle in my hands, I almost drop it on the wooden plank floor. Like playing a game of toss ball, it takes me three attempts to secure the bottle as I try to avoid eye contact with him.

There standing next to the table in all of his ripe and wonderful glory, is Lincoln. Naked as the day he was born, sans robe and sandals. He's tall, maybe six-two or three, with a body to die for. An Adonis. He's chiseled in all the right areas with an eight pack. My tongue would love nothing more than to dive right in those hills and valleys on display. He obviously takes pride in his body and the perfect v at the bottom of his stomach points directly to his large, oversized…

"Everly?" I can hear the mirth behind my name and it snaps me out of my daze.

"Huh?" My eyes slowly follow back up to his face.

"Back or stomach?" He grins, knowing the state he's just put me in.

Shaking my head, I cast my eyes down to the floor to get myself under control. This isn't the first time I've seen a naked man on my table, but this certainly is the first time I've ever lusted for a man about to get on my table.

"Sto—stomach." Good lord, this is going to be the longest four hours of my life and I'm just praying I can leave here with my virginity in tack.

He thankfully lifts the sheet and settles on the table facing down.

Starting with his feet, I decide that area will give me a chance to get myself back in order and calm down before the hard part comes and I have to flip him over. His soft moans aren't doing anything to calm the heat in the room and I think about turning up the a/c to cool things off. For some reason, I'm feeling a heatwave flowing through the room.

Lincoln starts to groan, as my fingers dig into the arch of his foot, and I swear I break out in a sweat. This is a bad idea. A very bad idea.

"Is there a specific place you want me to touch?" I babble on not really thinking before speaking.

Lincoln pops his head up, turning to face me.

"Oh, there are several places. I didn't realize happy endings were on the menu." He smirks and lets out a breathy chuckle.

Releasing his foot like it was a hot potato, I straighten up, placing both hands on my hips.

"That is NEVER on the menu," I forcefully say, aggravated that he would think that was something I did.

Lincoln clearly notices the change in me and shoots up from the table. I try my hardest to not look at his member, but definitely catch a glimpse of it as he tries to reach over to me. The grim look on his face tells me all I need to know.

"That was a poor attempt at a joke. Sorry if it offended you. I guess you bring out the immature teenager in me and I forget myself and my brain. Please forget I even said anything."

I know he didn't mean any harm. Hell, he's not the first one to ask about happy endings and I'm sure he won't be the last.

Quirking an eyebrow, I playfully shake my finger up at him.

"Don't do it again or I'll have Bubba come in to show you all about happy endings." I'm grinning by the end of my sentence and we both laugh.

"Bubba? Really?"

"He's our security guy who watches the monitors and walks around the building." I shrug.

Waving back towards the table, Lincoln turns and I watch his muscled butt retreat back to his spot on the table.

"I meant, do you have any areas that need more attention than others? Like your shoulders or lower back?" I resume my attention on his arch then switch to the other one.

He groans as he tells me his shoulders could use a little work then says, "You're really good at this," His voice is muffled as he's face down.

"Thanks, I've had years of practice."

Lincoln goes silent for a while as I make my way up his toned body. Every inch of this man is like a gift from God. He obviously takes pride in his workouts and what he eats. If you could create a perfectly sculpted body, this man right here would be the recipient of it. I can only imagine what his parents must look like.

The farther up his body I get, the more vocal he seems to be. The grunts, moans and groans have me checking the clock to see if our time is any closer to being done. I'm sweating up a storm and I'm finding it hard to keep my own moans to myself. My bottom lip is going to have a hole through it, as I keep clamping down on it to stop him from hearing me and my wayward thoughts.

"How do you feel so far?" I ask the usual question I ask all my clients.

"Fucking amazing," he murmurs.

Now comes my biggest challenge.

"Ready to turn over?"

"God, yes!" He almost falls off the table switching sides.

I'm not sure why he is so relieved until I see the very large tent pitching the sheet up in his mid-section.

"Oh," I can't stop the words from slipping through my lips.

"Ignore him if you can." I can hear the smile on his face but can't stop looking at his bulge.

I quickly turn my back to him, trying to calm myself and give me a few seconds to get my professional-self back in order. I know if he saw my face, he'd be able to tell just what I'm thinking.

"Would you like an eye mask? Some like to have them on when they're turned over to the back."

"Naw, I think I'd like to watch the master at work." He winks and my stomach does a flip.

How can one little gesture make me as nervous as a dog going in for a visit to the vet? Why do I feel like I have something to prove to this man? A man I only met twenty-four hours ago.

"So, Linc, what law firm do you practice at?" I ask but don't look up from his shins as I knead them with my fingers. I need to focus on the task at hand or I'll be distracted by other things going on with this handsome man on my table.

After a few groans he answers.

"Ahh, I work for myself at Thorne Law Firm. I started it about three years after completing law school. I did a few years as my father's shadow before venturing off and doing my own thing. When Levi passed the bar, he came along and joined me and the team."

Placing the sheet back over his lower leg, I move around the table and expose his other leg from under the thin fabric. I add more lotion on my hands and start to work above his ankle, giving him an excellent rub down.

"I like it."

"What?" I stop my fingers from going any farther.

"Linc. You call me Linc instead of Lincoln. Everyone calls me by my full name and I've always wanted it that way until you said it last night."

Thank God, I thought I might have said one of the several other names I've got rolling around my head at the moment. None of which are appropriate, and I'm sure my heated cheeks are giving it away.

As the minutes pass, I work my way up to his thigh. He's a lot more tense in these muscles as I try to focus on relaxing him and not on the large tent in the sheet that my hands are so close to. It continues to twitch as my own body flushes with heat. The thought of me being able to bring a man like him to this state boosts my confidence that I'm able to please a man.

"Are you okay?" I ask as he fidgets under my fingers.

"Ah," Linc doesn't say anymore but when I look up for more of an answer, he's staring straight at me with a look in his eyes. My eyes tune in and I'm lost. His blue eyes are a shade darker.

Linc's hands are holding onto the sides of the table as if they are a life raft in the middle of the ocean.

"Linc?"

"Stop. Touching. Me," his voice grits out and I'm taken aback and immediately take a step back.

Did I just cross a line?

CHAPTER FOUR

This woman has somehow managed to storm her way under my skin and consume me. And she doesn't even know it. Surely, she has to know the effect she has on me? I've all but professed it out loud. Not to mention, my body is physically showing her what she does to me when she's near.

She stirs something deep inside of me that I've never felt before. I spent all night stalking her. Trying to learn as much about her as possible. I finally gave up a few hours ago but before I settled into bed, called Ruby, my secretary, and had her make the necessary arrangements for this morning. Money talks in this city and it's a good thing I have a plethora of it. Ruby was able to clear all of Everly's appointments so that not only do I have her this morning but I'll have her all to myself until Monday. I've told Ruby to clear my calendar and not disturb me unless the company was on fire. Even then, I might send it to voicemail. Kevin was more than happy to take on my meetings and be on call until Tuesday. Olivia, my partner at the firm, sent a lengthy text wanting to know if I was in the hospital. She couldn't believe that I'd taken a day off.

Little does she know, I plan on spending a lot of time away from the office in the near future, if it means I can be with Everly. Or at least until I can permanently bind her to me. I wonder if she'd be interested in working only for me. I'd never get anything done if we were under the same roof during business hours, but I'd love to have her close every day.

The moment Everly placed her dainty, soft fingers on my body, she awoke something in me. It felt like a fire had been turned on and sends my body into a shockwave. Thank God I was on my stomach, just being in her presence sent all the blood rushing down to my very prominent, and favorite, body part. When she started rubbing me down, I think I was raised off the table at how hard my dick got. I was relieved when she asked me to turn over but then regretted it. The higher up she worked her magical hands, the closer I was to spewing my load under the sheet like a kid finding his first Playboy magazine.

The moment she turned around from getting the bottle of lotion from the cabinet earlier was priceless. I'm sure I'm not the first client to strut in naked but I sure as hell hope I'm the only one who has given her that response. She's the cutest, tiniest thing I've ever seen. I swear I could place her in my pocket, with how small she is.

I've never had a massage before and I think as long as she's the one doing it, I'll be a repeat customer.

"Are you okay?" I hear my angel ask but I'm trying to focus on anything other than her and how close her hands are to my cock.

I'm in the middle of the worst case of blue balls known to man and she seems completely oblivious to my *hardship*. She's either some witch who knows how to work a man into a tailspin, or she's the most innocent woman walking this earth. I'm hoping it's the latter.

I think I manage a grunt but as soon as she starts rubbing my inner thigh, I lose it. I'm pretty sure I say something but can't be quite positive as I feel precum pool at the top of my dick. I'm doing my best not to come but my body is on fire. I feel every nerve ending spark and if I don't calm the fuck down, I'm going to embarrass myself. Closing my eyes and inhaling in short controlled breaths, I manage to pull myself off the ledge. Why my body is acting like a teenage boy seeing a pair of tits for the first time is something I've never experienced in almost twenty years.

When I open them, the first thing I see are the most beautiful pair of hazel eyes staring back at me. They are wider than normal but still the most gorgeous set I've ever seen. She looks surprised, the more I take in her form, and my eyebrows shoot up. Immediately, I look down to make sure I didn't come but when I don't feel or see any wetness, I turn back to her.

"Everly?" I question as to why she's giving me a strange look.

She takes a few moments but then clears her throat. That's when I notice I've got both of her hands in one of mine, in a tight hold.

"We…we can…I can have someone else come in if you'd like." Her voice is a little shaky. But why?

I don't think I'll ever be able to have someone else massage me again. She's ruining me for all others.

"No, why would I want others when I've got you?"

She gives me a questionable look then shakes her head.

"But you just told me to stop touching you." Her eyebrows knit together and I try my best to think as to why I'd ever say something like that to her but remember just seconds ago I was doing everything in my power to not spew my load and faintly remember I did say something in the heat of the moment.

Leaning up from my back, I make sure not to release her

hands. The sheet falls from my hips exposing my favorite append-age and a pink blush, almost the color of her perfect lips, forms on her cheeks.

"I'm sorry I said that, angel. You seem to weave some type of spell on me that makes me lose all control, my body especially. If you'd continued your path, I think you'd have had a major clean up on your hands." I smirk when she understands where I'm going with this.

"Oh." Her mouth forms the perfect 'o,' and can't help but look down at my dick. "Mr. Thorne I'm going to need you to refrain from making any spills on my table please," she says very business-like as she tries to hold in the laughter.

"Maybe we should stay above the waistline for now." I wink and she greets me with a giggle, breaking character.

"Sure thing, boss." Her sass is something new and refreshing. Normally, I'd hate it coming out of a person's mouth but she's got this playfulness to her that separates her from the pack. Olivia, my business partner, gives me sass all the time but has no play-fulness to it, she's all business and no fun.

Finally releasing her delicate hands, she moves to the top of my head and lays me back down on the table. Her fingers work my scalp and if I didn't want to watch her, I'd be lulled to sleep.

"Tell me what brought you and your friends out to the bar last night," I say, trying to avoid plundering into a sleep cycle. Plus, I want to know all about her friends since her social media is locked down unless you do a friend request. I'm trying not to show my stalking skills too early and don't want to scare her away.

"Well, Saylor was meeting some old school buddies that were in town and dragged me along to meet them. She thought I'd like some of them."

There's more to the story, I can tell in the way her voice goes up and down. When I strolled over to their table it was mostly guys on the stools with only one other woman.

"She was trying to set you up," I state.

She swallows and moves her eyes upward letting out a sigh.

"Yeah, I guess you could call it a blind date or something."

The thought of her being set up with some stranger angers me. What if I'd not run into her at the courthouse? Would she have gone home with one of those losers?

"Guess we met at the right time then, huh."

She looks down and even though we are looking at each other upside down she still takes my breath away. Her smile could light up stadiums.

"I was definitely relieved you came over when you did. I thought you might stand me up."

"Never."

I can't stand it any longer. I've been restraining myself for far too long. She's had her hands all over me and I've been gripping the sides of the table, to not pull her to me.

"I'm going to kiss you."

I tell her but don't give her a chance to respond. Twisting, I pick up her petite body and angle her so she's face to face with me. She doesn't protest so I take that as a green light. We meet in the middle as our lips press together. Her warm, soft lips move along with mine as our tongues dance along to their own accord.

Before I know it, I've got her pinned under me on the table as I'm hovering over her. My elbows and knees take most of my weight so as not to crush her. She's a lot shorter than me but it's like we fit perfectly. Two puzzle pieces made for each other.

The room has soft music playing but all I hear is the quiet moans coming from her mouth.

"We…have to stop," Everly says in between our heavy make

out session but I'm having the hardest time finding the brakes. Only a sheet and her tiny ass shorts separate me from her little treasure box of heaven.

My hands are on her breasts and hers are on my chest but she's not pushing me away.

"Are you sure?" I pant and kiss my way down her jawline to her neck.

"Mhmm," she mumbles. "Someone could walk in. Doors don't have locks."

Like a bucket of cool water raining over me, I gather the strength of Hercules and pull away.

"We'll pick this up later at my place," I assure her, giving her one last kiss to hold us both over until then.

Everly's eyes have a dreamy glaze to them and I can't help but wonder if mine look the same to her.

Flexing to give her a show, I maneuver to lift up so she's able to move out from under me. As if that same cold bucket that fell on me got her too, she makes a show of straightening her clothes and hair.

"We shouldn't have done that." She's touching her kiss-swollen lips, trying not to smile. "I could be fired if someone had walked in. This is my job. My much-needed job and I can't be doing that."

"I agree and I'm sorry. Next time we'll have an appointment in my bed for a massage."

I can tell she's flustered as I swallow the chuckle caught in my throat. I'm not sure she's ever had someone so forward speak to her this way.

"This isn't funny, Linc." She practically stomps her heel. "I don't do this, you've…"

"I've what?"

I want to hear if I affect her the same as she does me.

"You, you manage to throw all the rules out the window."

BINGO!

Wrapping the thin sheet around my waist so that I'm not tempted to drive her into the wall for the entire spa to hear, I walk over to the end of the table where she's retreated to.

"You do the same for me, Everly. I've never been like this before and it's new territory for me too."

"I find that hard to believe. Look at you, women probably bow down at a chance with you."

She's got me there but I don't want to talk about other women. I want to focus on us and our future.

"You are all that matters to me. When I saw you yesterday, it did something to me. Something that I've never experienced before. It was like you called to me and I had to know who you were."

She looks as though she doesn't believe me and I don't blame her. I've just laid my cards on the table, hoping I haven't pushed too hard. Or scared the shit out of her.

"You have the power to crush me," she states, and I'm taken aback by the words. "I've never done this. Having people stick around for long periods of time is not something I've had a lot of experience with."

"Never done what? A relationship?"

She nods.

"Any of it. I've had a few short-term dates but as far as that, that's it. People don't tend to stay except for Saylor."

Mother of pearl, she's just been waiting for me to come and rescue her.

"I'd never crush or hurt you in any way," I say and cup her face with my hand tilting her face up to mine. "I'll make sure we take this nice and slow if you want. You can trust me and I'll prove it to you."

A buzzer goes off on the counter pulling us both out of our little bubble. Has it already been four hours?

Everly pulls away to turn it off. She starts putting the bottle of lotion up in the cabinet and the towels in the hamper.

"Other than a few hiccups what'd you think of getting a massage?" she asks as she starts to tidy the area.

"As long as it's your hands touching me, I think I might have my doctor recommend getting one twice a day."

"That good, huh?" she has her back to me but I can hear the amusement in her voice.

"Best I've ever had," I brag.

"I'll consider it a compliment even though I'm your first," she giggles.

"And last," I declare. "Let's go and have some lunch. I'd love to get to know you more."

She turns with a weary look, but the second she sees the sincerity in my face, her demeanor changes as I see the walls she's been building slowly begin to crumble. She might have a hard shell on the outside that is going to take some time to crack open and let me in, but I've got all the time in the world to chisel my way in. Not to mention I'm a master at negotiations.

"Okay."

CHAPTER FIVE

Yesterday was a whirlwind of events. After Linc and I went to lunch, we caught a movie and then walked around the beach for a bit. He truly seems like the perfect person, but no one can be that perfect. Saylor always says the first several months are like a honeymoon stage but then you really get to know each other after the first fight or a long separation. She's been in and out of relationships since we were teenagers. Her being older, I always watched her, hoping to one day have the confidence she showed.

Linc received a call last night as we were walking around from his business partner, Olivia, and had to head into the office. He was very pissed she couldn't handle whatever it was that was going on but after several minutes he ended the call looking flustered. He apologized but needed to head into the office to manage an employee that was handling a critical case. He followed me home in his car to make sure I made it there safely, then left in a rush with the promise to call me today.

Sundays are my cleaning and relaxing day but a message from Saylor tells me that I'm in for a day of pampering instead. She heard about my appointments being shifted to a big client and wants all the details. Even though she doesn't work there, she lives for the Hollywood gossip around here.

A few hours later, the apartment is tidy and all the laundry is done for the week. I've made a grocery list to pick up on my way home after hanging out with Saylor and checked my bills that are due to be paid for the month.

"Everly, you ready!" A loud knock startles me as I'm tying the laces to my white chucks. I've paired it with a ruffle strapless, loose summer top and denim capri worn jeans with holes throughout the legs.

"I'm ready," I answer the door, rolling my eyes. Saylor always pounds on my door like she's the police. She has a key to unlock the door, just as I have one for her apartment, but she loves to make me jump.

Saylor is in a short red romper that I'm sure if she bends just right, you'll see everything God gave her.

"So, are you going to spill or am I going to torture you to get all the details as to why you ditched me Friday night and all day yesterday after work?" she demands as we pull out of the parking garage, in her two door Mercedes red convertible. "I mean, Jesse was really into you and was disappointed when you left with that old guy at the bar."

Ever since meeting Saylor, I've tended to think that she falls on the more dramatic side of things, but I wouldn't have her any other way.

"Jesse seemed like a creep and had bad breath," I say and leave out that he wasn't the most attractive guy. I can deal with most things and look past their features if they have a good personality but lord, have some personal hygiene at least.

"Okay, no Jesse but what did you think about Mark?" She continues to question.

"Which one was he again?" I question not really remembering anyone but Linc.

"Oh Everly, what am I going to do with you?" Saylor gives an exasperated sigh. "Please tell me you finally got laid with that mysterious man you went across the street with, after leaving me all alone with my friends."

Eye rolling has become like second nature to me when I hang out with Saylor. Sometimes I swear she says things just to rile me up to get a reaction out of me. She knows all about the issues dad and I have had with my mother and how hard it is for me to connect with new people.

Leaving with Linc Friday night and going off with him yesterday was a big leap for me but something in me wants to be close with him. I can't really describe it, but I'm drawn to him for some reason, and I think he feels the same. But who am I to make that kind of judgement, I've never really had a real relationship and the short dates I've been on have only ended with making out.

"Earth to Everly!" Saylor interrupts my thoughts and brings me back. "Girl, you've got it bad. I've never seen you so smitten-kitten over a boy before."

"I'm not smitten-kitten, Saylor," I defend but really, I can't help but lie. I am smitten with Linc and can't stop thinking about him.

She rolls her eyes.

"Whatever you say."

"Did you stay all night at the bar or did y'all hit up another place after I left?" I ask.

"I stayed a little while after you left but then I met the most gorgeous man I've ever seen in my life."

"Really?"

"Really. I went to go and get the table refills on some beers, and he was sitting up on the stool watching the game with some buddies."

"Sounds like a normal Friday night for you," I joke, and she laughs with me.

"No, I'm telling you he was pur-fection," she gushes. "He paid for all the drinks I ordered and then we left."

"So, you didn't stay there with your friends?"

"No way. Girl, when prime rib is being dangled in front of you, you never settle for scraps," she says, and it makes me laugh. "Besides, he seemed a little on the quiet side so I thought going somewhere more private would be easier."

Our car ride isn't long and when I look up, I'm confused.

"Why are we at work on our day off? Isn't there some kind of rule for that or something?"

"Everly," she huffs. "This is a big deal for you, and I want to make sure you've got all your equipment finely tuned." Saylor gestures to my work building confusing me even more. The look I'm giving her must snap her out of her own head. "Grooming, Everly. Nails, hair, hedges—"

"Hedges?"

"Your bush." She points down at my vagina and I automatically cover the area with my hand, as if she was going to try and touch me. Saylor has no boundaries when it comes to the female anatomy, and I find myself fondled a lot when she's making references about my breast so I can just assume she wouldn't be any different with *that* area.

"It's trimmed," I adamantly state.

"Waxing is always better. Besides, you want to make sure you don't miss a spot, especially if he's eating your cookie."

Dear God, save me now.

I don't even reply because she'll just keep going and that's the last thing I want to be discussing. When we were teens, she was the one who gave me the *period talk.* Then not long after that, she told me all about the birds and the bees. Our dads were gone a lot on missions and her grandparents made sure we were taken care of during those times.

An hour later and after getting my hands and feet done, I'm laying down on a table in a treatment room waiting for one of my co-workers to come in and mangle my *very* private area, that only I've ever had access to.

The door opens and in walks one of my favorite people.

"I wondered when you'd finally come to me to have a good waxing," Christine says as she gloves up. "Saylor said to be gentle, as it's your first time. She also mentioned that you've got a man in your life now."

Christine is a really nice woman in her late thirties and has been with the spa since its opening. She's very motherly to all of us younger girls and treats us like her own four daughters at home.

I didn't grow up with a mother, but I had a lot of females surrounding me that stepped up and filled in when I needed it.

"Ugh! I don't really need this, I keep it nice and trimmed," I argue like a child. I know this hurts and why people put themselves through this is beyond me. The stories that they tell during our lunch breaks are hilarious but I'm worried that now I'm going to be one of them. "We could just talk for a while instead."

"Think of it as not having to shave as often and it won't cause those irritating red bumps."

Once she's got me in position and gloved up, I've changed my mind, but she's already splayed the wax to an area I'm sure is for doctor's eyes only. I massage clients all the time so I'm not shy when it comes to the naked body, but *my* naked body has only been seen by less than a handful of people walking this earth.

"Take a deep breath, honey."

I do as she says while my mind is yelling at me to run out the door and away from this room and to never look back.

"Maybe we should—" but before I can finish, Christine yanks the cloth strip and a scream shoots out of me involuntarily as my body moves to sit upright, in an attempt to bolt away from the source of pain. It sounds like a toddler getting a toy taken from them at daycare echoing from wall to wall. Tears form in my eyes; one breaches the lower lid and falls down towards my temple.

"Shh, it'll be okay," Christine says trying to sooth me but all I want to do is yell *liar* to her face. "The first one is always the worst." She tries to comfort me but continues to coat more wax on my southern lips. Newsflash, she doesn't look the least bit sorry.

"I'm good, we don't need to continue. I've got somewhere to be and—" She rips another and my entire body tenses to almost cramping status. "What is wrong with you! How can people want to do this!" I howl at her. My legs try to close, and I think I've gone lightheaded. The bright room starts to dim in and out and my focus is a little shaky.

"Almost done, honey, just a few more and then it's all over," Christine calmly says but I don't believe her. Not one little bit.

"Really? How many more?" I try to sound so hopeful. My hands are sweating, and I think I might have chipped a tooth bearing down with my teeth.

"Ah, maybe four?" She says like a question then rips off the next one. I wasn't focused and didn't even notice she'd slathered on more wax. I feel as though I'm numb from the waist down.

"Christine!" I yell this time and grab for her wrist. She's quick like a puma and moves before I can clamp down on her. She has a small smile that graces her face like she's hiding a secret or wanting to burst out in laughter. Any other time I'd probably be laughing my ass off if it were someone else but being the one on the table has me in agonizing tears. "I hate you right now."

"It's okay, honey. It'll all be worth it later."

She rips off the next one and the pain ebbs slightly. I must be in shock or have really gone numb down there; either way I welcome it. Why women do this is beyond me. Give me a razor and shaving cream and I'll die a happy lady. Maybe it's time the bush comes back in style.

Six rips later, yes, six and not the four she previously stated, Christine is applying aloe to my most tender and abused area of my body. All I can think about is how I'm going to murder Saylor, maybe I'll slip green hair coloring into her bowl as she gets her highlights after this. It'd serve her right.

After Christine goes over the aftercare, she leaves me to get dressed. I lay there on the table for a bit staring up at the ceiling wondering why we torture ourselves. There's a mirror in the corner of the room and as I'm locating my panties, I take a look at the damage. I'm still ruby red but I do have to admit that it does look much better than my own trimming. She still left a small strip at the top but everything else is smooth. *Irritated* but smooth.

I'll never admit this to Saylor or Christine but maybe it has its perks for waxing. Next time I should probably take some pain medicine beforehand.

Saylor: You still alive in there or should I call for medics?

Me: Coming, hold your horses! And I'm never talking to you again.

Saylor: You'll thank me when he's eatin'
that cookie!

Rolling my eyes at her text, I quickly but carefully dress then head out to meet up with my annoying best friend. She means only the best but sometimes I could strangle her for the things she gets me into.

CHAPTER SIX

Linc

Anne, the newest intern at the firm, brings me my tenth cup of coffee since last night. Olivia started blowing up my phone, calling me while I was on my date with Everly. After pushing her to voicemail for the sixth time, I finally answered. I wasn't happy about being interrupted but when she told me about what was going on, I knew I couldn't ignore it. My firm's reputation is everything to me and I'll be damned if I let some idiot ruin it for me.

Everly had been perfectly fine with wrapping up our date, but I hated that work was getting in the way of us getting to know each other. I'd learned so much about her and was clueing in on her little ticks as the day went on. When she would get nervous, she'd wring her hands or bite that delicious lip. Her go-to sign is when she rubs her forehead. At the movies, we held hands and snuck several make out sessions in like we were teenagers in high school. I felt so carefree and young again, especially since I haven't been to a movie in over a decade. Sure, I'd been to a lot of movie premieres to get my face, and the firm's name, out there but I'd never stay and watch what was showing.

She has this personality to her that draws people in. Her easy-going, bubbly attitude is something that catches everyone's eye. Even the eyes of other men who I want to put my fist through their teeth. We were at the refreshment counter getting popcorn and drinks when the little high school boy tried hitting on her. Right in front of me. Of course, Everly just thought he was being friendly, but I knew right then that I'd need to rein in my temper. No way was I going to jail over beating up a seventeen-year-old. But I sure did make a show of wrapping an arm around her waist and nipping her neck right there for that boy to see. She doesn't even notice the attention and when I asked her when we found our seats, she was shocked that the boy was hitting on her. How can a gorgeous woman like her not see this?

"Tell me about your family," she asks as we share a plate of hot wings.

"My parents died when Levi and I were young. We came to live with our aunt and uncle, here in California."

"That's horrible, Linc. Can I ask how they died?"

"When I was eleven, my two-year-old sister was killed. According to the police reports, my mother had left the front door to our apartment open as she was bringing in groceries from the car. My sister, Maggie, wandered out and was struck and killed by a car driving by. Levi, who was four at the time, almost got hit too. Mom was never the same after that."

"Oh, I can't even begin to imagine what your mom went through."

"We didn't live in the best complex and she was easily able to numb her pain with drugs. My dad followed shortly behind her; he never came right out and blamed her for Maggie dying, but everyone knew he did. For three years they let their grief consume them, never once concerned with mine or Levi's well-being. They didn't even notice we lived in the same apartment most of the time. Over those years, neither parent could hold down a job for long; they were either too high or didn't care enough to show up to get paid. Soon, the money started to cease coming in and mom and dad began pawning off our belongings to be able to pay for their next fix. One day, Levi and I came home from school and found them both passed out on the floor in the empty living room. Only they weren't passed out; they'd overdosed from a bad batch of heroin. At least that's what I overheard one of the cops say."

Her gasps bring me back from those dark memories. Some days feel like it was just yesterday that I opened the front door and saw them there.

"Child Protective Services came in and took us out, placing us both in the foster care system. They searched for our next of kin but it took some time to find. Both of my parents had left their families and took off, never looking behind. They met in Seattle, Washington and started a life without ever contacting relatives."

"I'm so glad you were able to reconnect with your aunt and uncle," she offers.

"We were born up in Washington and didn't even know we had other family. Then after they passed, we found out we had a lot more family. We met Daniel and Alice, who we call mom and dad, but also Reid, who is my age. Then we were introduced to my grandparents. They were shocked that their son had an entire family that they never knew about."

"Wow, I'm sorry they passed."

I shrug as if it's not a big deal. I doubt she'd want to hear all about my woos of growing up, trying to please everyone in the family so that I'd be loved and not abandoned.

"It was a long time ago." I lean back in my chair. "What about you? Tell me about yours."

"I'm pretty simple," she gives me the same shrug that I gave earlier. "My dad is—or was in the military so I was a MB."

"MB?"

She chuckles, "Military brat. We moved a lot over the years, to different bases, all over the world. I was so thankful for Saylor because where my dad went so did her dad."

"And your mom?"

"Ah, she didn't like being bounced around, so when I was nine she packed up and left. I haven't spoken to her since. She's never called or written—nothing."

"How did your dad manage to leave on missions, with you not having family there to watch over you?"

"Saylor's grandparents, Sharolyn and Alan, who own the spas, took temporary custody of me while dad was gone. They were there when Robin left dad and I." I notice she calls her mom by her legal name. "Saylor pleaded for them to keep me. Saylor's mom had passed away from cancer and was having a hard time with everything so they came to an arrangement with my dad so that he could continue to be an active soldier with his unit."

I feel like we have a lot in common, when it comes to abandonment from immediate family. The more I learn the more I see how much not having them in your life can affect a child and their future because of certain choices the adults make.

"Are you close with your grandparents?" she asks.

My lips twitch at the mention of them. "Yeah, at least I try to be. We try to speak at least once a week and check in," I say and pop a fry in my mouth. "They're getting older and spend more time in Montana now at the small ranch all of us go to during holidays."

"It's such a small world because Saylor's grandparents also have a place out in Montana. They spend the majority of the year out there in their little town now that they're getting older."

"What city do they have a place in, do you remember?" I ask.

"We go up there once a year to visit with them. They live in Dillon. It's beautiful until winter comes, then I'm ready to get back here to thaw out." She giggles and I follow suit.

"I'm the same. I don't mind a little cold but only when I go skiing. Grandpa and Grandma have a place a town or two over from Dillon called Twin Bridges. We've had to fly into Dillon a few times or I wouldn't know that city."

"Did you speak with Bill in HR?" Olivia breaks me out of my thoughts coming into my corner office with a stack of more papers. She looks just as tired as I am. We haven't had to pull all-nighters since law school and it's starting to weigh on my mental state.

I shake my head and sip on the hot coffee. The burn tunneling down my throat only soothes me, as I feel as though I'm on fire, after learning of this betrayal in my own company.

"I want everything we have so there won't be any surprises to find out about later on. He obviously wanted us to be blindsided when this was submitted in court." My conference table by the windows is filled with boxes of evidence and witness statements for our high-profile case with Dustin Barker.

Dustin Barker is being tried for the murder of his former girlfriend and her lover. There is the murder weapon with his fingerprints on it and also bloody clothes that match the victims' blood type. It should be a no brainer for the prosecution, but the chain of evidence and command has been improperly followed along with some other evidence that looks to be planted, not to mention protocol wasn't followed by a new officer on the force. We took on the case when his father, who is part owner in an oil company, came to us for our help. We knew it wouldn't be a slam dunk but that makes the challenge sweeter. That and the hefty payment that hit our account.

I wasn't the lead attorney on the case, but I've been involved the entire time. I've had several other cases I'm working on right now and set Kevin Jenkins as the lead. He was promoted two months ago as a Senior Associate and has moved up in the ranks quickly. Kevin has one of the best win records out of the associates and works harder than anyone else in the firm, except Olivia and me. He has a lot of potential which is why I can't seem to wrap my head around what we've recently found out.

"It just doesn't make any sense. Why would he ruin his career like this? It's kind of a no brainer with the case," Olivia voices to no one in general.

"I'm just glad Alex thought enough to double check the statements before court on Wednesday. This could do a lot of damage to the firm once it was submitted."

"Yeah, we lucked out with that one. Maybe we should designate a person who looks over all the paperwork before submitting," I say thinking out loud.

"It's not a bad idea but we'd need more than one person with as many cases as we have going on," Olivia adds.

"Let's ask Bill in HR what his thoughts are and Sally over in financing if it's something we can do as a trial basis," I say and send off a quick email to them inquiring about our current needs. "Have you called Kevin in yet?"

"No, I wanted to make sure we had all our ducks in a row."

We spend the next five hours poring over the documents, finding more and more falsified statements. Kevin really wanted to stick it to us, or me I should say. Almost every document that is falsified is signed and dated under my name, even though I have not done much with this case. If this had been found out by the court and or the prosecutors, I could be disbarred and lose my law license here in California. No way in hell am I going to lose something I've worked my ass off to get to where I am. Not to mention, the state could open up all my previous cases to make sure there wasn't any foul play in the past as well. In other words, it would fuck my life up even more and it wouldn't be pleasant for any of my former clients.

The more I find, the angrier I get. This piece of shit was trying to set me up to take a huge fall. I've had Dean, our researcher and investigator for the firm, come and start doing a more thorough background on Kevin Jenkins, to see what this dude's problem is. Why is he willing to throw away years of hard work and school for this?

A knock on my door has me looking up from the papers in front of me. Dale, my security, stands there with a duffle bag. I'm still in the clothes I wore yesterday, when I went out with Everly to the movies. Christ, I haven't even slept yet as the twenty-four-hour mark has approached. Olivia went home a few hours ago to get some rest before coming in early tomorrow morning for the confrontation with Kevin.

Checking out the window, it's pitch black, and my eyes are getting blurry as the words are all mushing together. My head hurts from wanting to explode and strangle my soon-to-be former employee, and I think I need to call it a night.

"Dale," I address him. "Let's get out of here. Take me home, please."

The moment I go to stand, I feel every bit my age as the stiffness from sitting too long kicks in and I walk as though I'm in my eighties.

In the car, I shoot off more emails to HR about Kevin and

then check my texts. I haven't heard anything from Everly today and hate that this shithead ruined my weekend with my girl.

Me: You still up, angel?

I check my watch seeing that it's clearly after eleven.

Everly: Watching a movie.

Everly: Did everything go okay with your case?

My chest tightens with her asking about it.

Me: As good as could be expected. Have lunch with me tomorrow.

It takes a few moments, and I think she might've fallen asleep but the dots start to pulse. I know she's off on Mondays and she'd told me earlier that she didn't have any plans, so this is perfect.

Everly: You aren't busy? Tomorrow is Monday. Like a normal workday for most people.

I actually laugh and it feels good after the past twenty-four hours I've had.

Me: I'll always make time for you.

Everly: Okay, but I'm picking this time. Should we meet somewhere?

Me: Come to my office around noon.

I shoot off the address and feel the bubble back in my stomach when I'm around her.

Everly: See you then.

Yes you will, babe.

I'm back in the office before the sun is up, running on only a few hours of sleep. Every time I'd close my eyes, I kept replaying all the documents I've scoured over. What in the actual fuck is wrong with Kevin?

It's after nine and Olivia and I just finished a consultation with an outside source to help us navigate through this when Ruby tells me that Kevin is here. Our consultant, who's been an attorney for over forty years, advised us to not only fire him for the documents but turn him over to the law board to have his law license revoked. There was nothing criminally we could do, as he didn't turn them over to the courts yet, but that still doesn't mean we can't threaten it.

"Send him in Ruby," I reply back to her. We have Bill, from HR, here with us to make sure we follow the proper procedure. Dale is also lingering around, in case this shithead decides to go postal on us.

"You ready for this?" Olivia asks as the door opens and Kevin strolls in as if he doesn't have a care in the world.

"Morning," Kevin greets as he takes a seat next to Olivia, in my butter soft leather chair. He has no idea that we're on to him and it makes this even better. I know I should be on high alert that we've got a fox in the hen house and that we only caught this just days before it was to be submitted. He's making it hard not to punch him through my glass window and have him fall the fifteen floors down to the busy street.

Olivia raises an eyebrow, then gets up and takes her place in a chair on my side of the desk next to me, facing him. We usually sit this way when we interview new attorneys or when review time comes around annually, so the prick probably thinks he's getting promoted again.

Fucker.

Clearing my throat to make sure my voice is steady and level, "It has come to the attention of our firm that an issue has come up on the Barker case from one of the associates," I say. I want to see his reaction when all this unfolds.

"Issue?" He repeats. "What kind of issue?"

"Yes, and we think it's in our best interest to remove you from the case effective immediately," Olivia adds. She is on the same page as me and wants the shit-stain to squirm a little. He probably thinks this is some kind of sexual harassment thing with another employee or something.

"I'm not sure what issue you're talking—" he starts to say but I stand and gather the copies of documents that he's falsified.

Kevin instantly goes sheet white when he starts to scan over the documents. Gotcha fucker. But he quickly regroups.

"I'm not sure what all this is but I can assure you that it must be one of the other associates on the case." His hands are slightly shaking against the documents he's holding but he's doing everything in his power to gain some kind of control over his body.

"Really?" I question. "Who do you think?" I act like I'm giving him a chance to pin this on someone else. The little weasel. "Someone is trying very hard to ruin my reputation and end my law career by doing this."

"I'm not sure but I can say that it wasn't me," Kevin defends. "I've worked my butt off to get where I am in the firm."

"That's really interesting Kevin," Olivia voices and then turns the open laptop around to face him. "This is the company computer that was issued to you four months ago, is it not?" Olivia points to the code on the laptop, then to the copy of HR's records.

He sits there still as a statue, and I know he's trying to think of a way to argue out of this. I would.

"We also had IT come in over the weekend to show us the footage of when the saved files of the false documents were created and saved. They all show you on this computer at the time." I turn my monitor around with the security footage of those dates and times.

We have cameras on all four floors of our offices. There isn't audio because of attorney/client privilege but we do have security cameras that record everyone's movements. We had a case two years ago where a man came into our offices with a gun after we'd won a huge case in court. He didn't even have anything to do with the case but was just a bystander who was upset that it didn't go the way he thought it should. Needless to say, we've upped our security to a topnotch system that covers every inch of this place.

That is also one of the reasons Dale is by my side most of the time. He came after I was attacked in the parking lot of the courthouse. Olivia has her own too, but she prefers them to remain in the shadows and she doesn't take the higher profile cases that don't make the news like most of mine do.

"We plan to report this activity to the law board as well as our state department—" Olivia begins to say.

Something flashes in Kevin's eyes like the calm before the storm. He knows he's been made and is backed into a corner. Bill starts to speak and all of us know the end is near, but Kevin jumps up from his seat, making Olivia flinch, then leans back in her chair.

"You think you're so untouchable," he spews looking right back at me, becoming unhinged at the drop of a hat. I just sit there and let the man say whatever it is he wants. This isn't the first person who wanted to tell me off, but this is the first person who works for me that's tried to set me up. "Your day is coming, Lincoln; the apple doesn't fall far from the tree."

What an odd thing to say?

He continues his rant for a good couple of minutes before he realizes that we're not going to engage with him. In a last-ditch effort, Kevin sweeps his arms, clearing my desk of all its items, before Dale and another security member come from the doorway to escort him out. Dale has him by the elbow, almost to the door, when Kevin shrugs him off, giving him a shove. Kevin starts to deck Dale but of course Dale is quick on his feet and clocks him across the cheek, sending him sailing against the wall.

Dale and the other security officer both collect Kevin off the wall and escort him out of the room and down the hall. Kevin is manically laughing and yelling how he's going to ruin my life and everything in it. The guy has officially lost his marbles.

"That was interesting," Bill says as he gathers his papers. "I'll have all his belongings sent to the address listed in his file. My advice is to not engage in any discussions with him or about him with any other employee here at the firm." *As if I'd even mention that shithead's name.* "I'd also suggest that you file for a restraining order to keep him off the property." With that last parting gift he's out the door.

"Well, that went better than I expected," Olivia sarcastically mumbles as she starts to pick up the items on the floor.

"The guy's a total lunatic." I bend down, retrieving the monitor and keyboard along with my laptop and papers that are scattered amongst the mess. "How'd we not see how crazy the guy was? Let's get a few interns and junior associates to go through his past workload and report back to us. Hopefully, this was the first time he'd done something like this."

"Mr. Thorne, Linley Lewis is in the lobby trying to gain access.

She doesn't have an appointment to see you but she's insisting," Ruby speaks over the phone intercom that's still on the floor next to my desk.

Christ, can't I catch a break today? My temple throbs at the mention of her.

"I'll go down to the lobby and speak with her, don't let her up." I bend down, picking the phone up and placing it back where it should be. Checking my watch, I see that it's almost time for Everly to stop by for lunch. At least my day is about to get better.

"Ah, so the beautiful Linley Lewis is back in town," Olivia jokes. "So, she's the one that made you want to take time off."

Her words make me want to vomit. Linley Lewis is the last person I'd rearrange my schedule for. Which reminds me.

"Ruby, please make sure Everly Bryant is always put through to me and given access to my office. She actually should be here soon."

"Yes, Mr. Thorne, I'll let Briana down in the lobby know."

"Thanks Ruby."

"Everly? I thought Linley was the fling of the season."

I ignore her comment and put the finishing touches on the last few items on my desk.

"Let me guess, she's the newest model of Ms. Hutchins' modeling agency." Olivia continues to probe. I can hear the distaste in her voice at the mention of Blaire Hutchins.

I hate talking about my personal life with people. Especially those I work with. I'm usually in the gossip mill with a model on my arm and everyone just assumes we're in a relationship. What they don't know is they are completely wrong. I'd never want to be tied down to those shallow people.

"I'll take your silence as a yes," Olivia boasts like she just figured out an unsolvable problem.

"You are wrong counselor and are getting colder by the second."

"Really? Because I'm usually spot on with you and your… ladies." She raises an eyebrow, egging me on to confirm that she's not wrong.

"Completely wrong *this* time," I say as she props herself up on the edge of my tidy desk like I'm going to cure the world of cancer in my next words, and it irritates me. "Ahh, fine. I met Everly the other day at the courthouse after we won."

"The one you spoke to before we had our media conference? The one you joked about being your future wife?" She laughs then sees the seriousness on my face. I think I've shocked her because she's looking at me as if I belong in the psych ward.

"Yes, that's her."

Olivia stares at me for a second, looking over my face trying to read me like a book or tarot cards.

"You more than hit it off if you were going to rearrange your schedule for today, had the Kevin situation not come up. Lincoln, you never take days off and after meeting a woman for all of five minutes you're calling in *sick*. She's special. So where does Linley fit in all this?"

"She doesn't. Linley is probably back in town, wanting me to look over some new contracts for her." Locking up the last of my things in my top drawer, I turn back to Olivia ready for this interrogation to be over. When I'm ready to share Everly, I will. "Is there anything else you need, or can you hold down the fort for the rest of the day?"

She gives me a curious but satisfying look, then nods.

"Do I at least get to meet her?" Olivia asks as we walk out of my office, she trails me to the elevator.

The doors open and Levi walks off. I block the entrance,

keeping her out and from coming down to the lobby to scope out Everly. Levi has turned around and is giving us a confused look.

"You'll meet her when I'm ready for everyone to meet her. She's all mine and I don't want to scare her off with the likes of you and your interrogations," I say. Olivia's a great person. Pushy as hell but a great person.

"Fine, but I expect to be the first one to meet her." She plants her hands on her hips. "Even before Reid and this guy." She points over at Levi.

"Hey, I'm blood," he counters, piping in, even though he has no clue what we are even talking about.

"We'll see," I quickly say as the doors close, leaving me alone as the elevators descend. Technically, Levi and Reid didn't get to meet Everly at the bar Friday night so I think I'm covered for now.

When I reach the lobby, the rotating door catches my eyes as my angel walks in, in a denim romper with brown wedges. Her hair is curled in soft waves, she's still short in the tall shoes but her legs look like they go on for days. She looks perfect. Like the magnets we are, our bodies start to gravitate towards each other. I'm sure the lustful look on my face says it all to everyone passing by but I don't care. I'm almost to her when some blonde blocks my sight of Everly and wraps around me.

"Surprise!" I hear and feel a pair of lips pressed against the crease of my lip. Thank God I was able to dodge her or else she'd have caught my full lips.

Extracting her from my chest, I hold her at arm's length at the tops of her bony shoulders.

"What are you doing?" I ask as I stare down at Linley in confusion.

"I'm here to surprise you, silly," she says like I'm supposed to know what she means. "I got back in last night and thought you'd want to see me." She tries to maneuver out from my grip and wrap her arms back around me but I hold firm not letting her move an inch.

I peek over her shoulder and watch as Everly looks crushed as she glances back and forth between the two of us at a distance. She starts to back away from the lobby and towards the glass door at the entrance.

Not going to happen.

Pushing off of Linley and ignoring her completely, I stride over to Everly and engulf her in a bear hug with my chest against her back. She goes ridged in my arms and doesn't move to hug me back or touch me with her hands. Leaning down so that my lips are next to her ear I speak softly.

"She's a client." I give the best explanation I can without having to hash out my past with Linley here in the lobby.

"Do all of your clients greet you that way?" She grits out. I can actually hear her teeth grinding as she tries to pry my hands off her.

Turning her around to face me, I see hurt in her eyes but also jealousy and for some reason I love it. It means she's just as interested in me as I am with her.

"Linley and I…"

"Ah, excuse me!" I hear a high-pitched voice like nails on a chalkboard. We both turn to the noise and see Linley standing there with her hands on her hips and narrowing eyes. "What the hell is going on here?"

Everly stiffens even more, and I tighten my hold on her.

"Everly this is Linley Lewis, a client. Ms. Lewis this my girlfriend, Everly," I announce. Surely, Linley will get the hint and take a hike leaving us alone, but Linley was never the brightest light in the room, and she'd never skip the chance to draw in drama.

She lives by the rule that all media attention is great for her career, good or bad.

"Girlfriend? I'm gone for a month and already I've been replaced by," Linley's eyes scrutinize Everly from the top of her head to the tip of her toes. "Her?" she says the word like it's dirty and I want to have her thrown out of the building on her ass.

"Ms. Lewis I'd suggest you make an appointment if you're wanting to discuss your modeling contracts otherwise you have no business here and need to leave."

"I'm more than a client and you know it, Lincoln." She bites back. "She's not even like the rest of us, she's short and thick."

Linley would think a straw was thick, as she thinks eating is for fat people. You can strip her naked and count every one of her bones with how obscenely skinny her frame is.

"That's enough, Ms. Lewis. If you aren't here for business, I'll have you escorted out."

"Ha, have your fun but I'll wait for a call when you're done poking the pork," she sneers and storms out of the building.

It takes a second to calm myself and not run after Linley to toss her out myself, but I manage to hang onto Everly and remember she's much better to be around than that vapid bitch who just vacated the building.

"I'm sorry about that," I start to say but Everly holds her hands up stopping me.

"You know, I forgot I've got a training thing at work and need to get going." She starts to turn and leave the same way Linley just exited, but I catch her elbow, stopping her in her tracks.

"No, you don't. Let's go have some lunch and talk. Give me a chance to explain what just happened." She doesn't look convinced. "Please." I tuck a strand of hair behind her ear and lift her chin with my finger.

She takes a step back and gives me a hard look shaking her head.

"Listen, I'm not into "other women" drama. If you and she are an item, or even on the cusp of any type of relationship, then I'm out. I've learned a lot over the last three years from clients and friends, and I don't want any of that in my life. I get that this is Hollywood, and gossip sells but I refuse to be put in a position where I'm splashed across the media in a negative way."

"There is nothing going on with Ms. Lewis and I. I'm not even sure why she thought we were a thing," I say. "Let's head out like we planned and have some lunch."

Finally, after she wrings her hands looking around the lobby she says, "Okay but I meant what I said. No drama, Linc."

CHAPTER SEVEN

Everly

Warning Bells!! Red Flags!!

What am I doing? I should just walk out of here and not look back. I knew things were too good to be true. And to think I just endured getting my own flesh being ripped off my body to cleanse itself from unwanted hair.

Could she be just a client? She looks so familiar, but I can't quite put my finger on it. It would be right to give him the benefit of the doubt but after the little stunt Linley just pulled, I'm hesitant. She seemed a little too familiar with Linc to just be a client, but I guess I'll find out over lunch.

We walk together with our hands entwined, because Linc refuses to release his hold on me, through the revolving glass doors of his building and out in the LA sun. It's a beautiful day out and I'm hoping that it wasn't just ruined.

"Where would you like to eat lunch?" He asks, placing sunglasses on to shield his eyes.

He looks amazing in a fitted dark gray suit and tight black

shirt underneath. He's got a slight stubble on his face that makes him even more handsome.

"I guess that depends on how much time you've got to eat," I offer as we stand on the curb as people stroll by us.

"The rest of the day is all yours, angel. I'm at your mercy." He bends down a touch like he's bowing to royalty, and I can't help the laugh that escapes my lips. He really is funny sometimes.

"I hope you're adventurous when it comes to eating."

"I've got a stomach of steel!" He pats his belly then grabs for my fingers again. "Lead the way."

We walk down a few blocks to the small park where the parking lot is full of people on their lunch break. Linc has taken off his suit jacket and rolled up his sleeves, bearing his muscled forearms. I've touched over almost every inch of this man's body and have each part of his glorious frame memorized after Saturday's massage.

As we approach the park, Linc is still looking around trying to figure out which restaurant we're going to, and I hope he's not too disappointed in my choice. I know he's used to the finer dining and mainstream eating establishments and there's nothing wrong with that; it's just sometimes your body needs some hearty junk.

"Well, are you in the mood for tacos, waffles or maybe turkey legs?"

Linc's eyebrows crease as he ponders over my selections.

"Are we headed to a carnival?" he questions, and it makes me laugh.

I wave my hand over to the food trucks at the park and his mouth drops open, then closes like a fish.

"I… we… ah," I think for the first time ever I've just shocked him speechless.

"Ever eaten off a food truck before?"

"Is it even safe to eat that food? Aren't there like rules and regulations about this?" He continues to stare over at the truck, completely missing the line of people who enjoy this every day.

"It's not as bad as you think," I coax. "And I thought you said you liked to do adventurous things?"

"Not as bad? Don't people get food poisoning from these places? I can see the growing number of lawsuits as we watch them stuff their faces, Everly," he says so matter of fact.

Now I do erupt in laughter that makes others turn towards us.

"Don't knock it, till you've tried it. Come on, don't be so judgmental, food trucks are under health code regulations too."

I'm dragging Linc across the parking lot, getting in line at the taco truck. Saylor and I come here and eat when we can, they have the best tacos. Once we've made it to the front of the line, I order four tacos and two waters.

"I'm not looking forward to getting my stomach pumped in a few hours," Linc grumbles, snagging some napkins.

"Don't worry, I'll be right by your side holding your hand if you do," I say and nudge the taco towards his mouth as we sit under a shade tree having a makeshift picnic.

As the first bite is chewed and swallowed, Linc seems to finally come around. His eyes roll back as he hums his appreciation for them.

"Oh my God, that's good. That's really good." He continues to stuff his face and hum after every bite. "How did I ever think this was horrible?"

"Sometimes you've got to take a chance," I respond and wipe my mouth with a napkin.

Linc pauses for a second with a taco midair and has a twinkle in his soft blue eyes.

"I couldn't agree with you more." He smirks then demolishes the other taco.

Linc takes the trash and tosses it in the bin then comes back to sit down, pulling me into his lap. He kisses me on the temple, and I think it's time for that explanation from earlier.

"So, are we going to talk about what happened in the lobby, or what?"

He releases a long breath before turning me to face him.

"Linley is a model who I met through an acquaintance, who happens to be another client, and took to a few functions. I needed a date, and she loved being photographed in public on the arm of a public figure."

"Huh." Is the only thing I can think of at the moment as I take in what he's just told me. If he's used to dating models then what in the hell is he doing with me? "So how long were you two dating?"

"Dating? No, we never dated. We went to four functions over the course of two months and that was it. We never went on a sit down, isolated date. You'll never see any photos of us walking in the park or coming out of a restaurant or shopping together. We only did functions, then went our separate ways. I haven't even seen her in over a month."

"So, she's like rent-a-date or something? I'm confused as to why someone would want to have an arrangement like this."

Linc stares blankly at me for a minute and then tosses back the rest of his water.

"I'm not sure why she reacted the way she did. I can assure you that there is no comparison to what I've felt with you, to any-one else I've ever had in my life Everly. No one. She's not, nor has she ever been, my girlfriend. In fact, the last time I had a girlfriend was like freshman year of college, fifteen years ago."

I'm sure he can see my wheels turning, trying to process his words.

"I promise, Everly, you are the only woman in my life and the only woman I want in it."

"Okay," I say and let the rest go, even though Linley's reaction was saying something totally different. He's given me no reason not to trust him at this point and until then I have to trust that what he's saying is the truth. There still seems to be more to this Linley situation but now is not the time to delve into it. *Why ruin a perfectly good day on the past, right?*

He leans in and captures my lips to his in a soft but needy kiss. Almost like we're sealing the deal on something. We only pull away when we hear the voice of a tiny person.

"Gross, ew! You're gonna get cooties from that!" a little boy says as he grabs the soccer ball that's rolled next to us on the grass. He couldn't be more than five years old.

"Trust me kid, in ten years you're going to love swapping spit with girls," Linc says deadpan and I try to hide my belly laugh.

The little boy scrunches his face then takes off running with his ball in his arms.

"You probably just scarred the poor boy for the rest of his childhood." I laugh and lean in to kiss him again, only to stop right before our lips connect. "Wait, what if he's right and you have cooties?" I start to back away in a dramatic manner, but Linc is right there to hold me in place with his fingers threaded through my locks.

"Then that's something we'll have to deal with together."

Linc shifts his hands in my hair and guides my face to his, never losing eye contact. Once we're nose to nose, he presses our lips together and I get lost once again in his soft touch.

"Now, what else did you have planned for the rest of the day for us?" Linc asks when we pull away leaving me breathless.

"Oh, well, I thought you had to get back to work so this was pretty much it."

Most people can't just leave in the middle of a Monday, so I didn't have anything else in mind.

Linc reaches into his jacket, pulling out his phone and starts typing something while smiling the entire time.

"I think I've got just the thing for us to do."

CHAPTER EIGHT

I message Dale, my security, the plans and type everything I need. I really want to spend as much time as I can with Everly and make the most of it, so enlisting Dale to help will free up some of that time. I've told him to pick up some beach clothes for myself and Everly and anything else we might need for the rest of the day. Hopefully, he was able to handle the Kevin situation quietly so as to not alert the other associates. I'd hate for it to get out, causing the rumor mill to ignite like wildfire.

Dale arrives thirty minutes later with a change of clothes for me at the food trucks, after I devoured another three tacos while waiting for him. My mind has been changed on food trucks and everything I ever thought about them. Maybe I can have the truck set up outside my building and offer lunch to the staff one day. Huh. Or maybe I'll keep this little treasure all to myself and I'll be able to sneak away for lunch, from time to time, to get out of the office for a bit. I definitely need to let Levi in on this food area.

"Are you going to let me know where you're taking me?" Everly asks when we head west on the highway.

I can't help but smile. I've come to know that she hates sur-prises but that's one thing she's going to have to get over because I plan on surprising her as often as possible.

"Thought we could hang out around the Santa Monica Pier."

When her eyes light up, I know I made the right choice. I've spent the last eight years working my ass off, growing my firm into what it is now, and I think I've earned a little reprieve.

We spend the rest of the day and evening along the pier play-ing games, riding the carousel and roller coaster. We eat burg-ers and fries, then have ice cream while walking on the beach. Everything seems easy with Everly. We talk and laugh and it's like I'm this young kid experiencing life for the first time. She brings out the kid in me that's been hidden for so long under briefings and court cases.

On our way back to Beverly Hills we cuddle in the back seat, stealing little kisses and touches while Dale drives down the high-way. It's as if our parents are driving us back from a date and we're trying to not get caught. *The things this woman makes me feel.*

All too soon we arrive back at her apartment. Dale pulls up to the curb and places the car in park.

"Did you want to come up for a bit?" She bites her lush bot-tom lip that I've nipped at during the drive home.

As much as I'd love to go upstairs, I can't quite bring myself into trusting what I'd do with her alone. We've only just met a few days ago and I know from watching and hearing her talk that she's not ready for what my body wants to do to her.

"I'd love to but not tonight." Her face drops in disappoint-ment and my chest tightens. She does her best to recover at the rejection but I'm doing this for the both of us. Lifting her chin so that her hazel eyes are staring back at me, I say, "I've got court first thing in the morning and need a good night's rest. Some of us mere mortals need all the beauty rest we can get."

She rolls her eyes and the area below my belt sets on fire. Most of my blood already shifts southward when she's around but this is something else.

"You know, we used to get swatted as kids when we rolled our eyes," I tell her and give her some insight into being brought up with my family.

"Oh really?" Everly gets a look in her eye and a mischievous grin on her face. "So, is that what you'll do if I roll mine? Spank me?"

"Well, it's never too early to learn basic manners, baby. Grandma was very adamant about us not being raised up as delinquents."

There's a fire of lust in her eyes and if I don't stop all this talk about spankings then I might actually give in, throw her over my shoulder and caveman walk her all the way up to her place.

So instead, I lean into her ear and whisper, "You're playing with fire, angel." My lips lightly bite her lobe and the low moan and hitched breath from her makes my dick jerk. She's almost in my lap and if the sight of Dale exiting the car wasn't like a gush of cold water reminding me that we're in a parked car at the curb of a busy street, I'd lay her down and give her what her body is so desperately needing and begging for.

Reaching around her, my hand clicks the handle on the door and the interior lights invade the darkness. With a peck on my cheek, Everly gathers her stuff and moves out of the car and onto the curb of her apartment entrance. Not wanting to be left with only a peck, I climb out of the car and in a few strides, I've swung her around so that I've boxed her in at the glass door of her apartment entrance.

"Did you think a peck would satisfy me until next time?" Her smirk says that she's got me right where she wants, and for some reason I'm okay with that.

"Thought you might be in a hurry to get home for that beauty sleep," she coyly says. Everly is the first woman I don't mind playing games with. Our banter is refreshing, and I love it. She makes me work for every inch of her and isn't one to throw herself at me to get any monetary or media notoriety.

I hover over her as I bend down to capture those plump lips. With one arm wrapped around her tiny waist pulling her even closer to me, the other is still flat on the glass. I'm lost in the moment until I hear the sound of footsteps and the noise of someone annoying clearing their throat. Everly is either lost in the moment and doesn't hear them or just doesn't care as I slide us over from the front of the door to the side, letting the person move by. Fixating back on my angel, I can hear the mutter of the person mention getting a room or something, but I don't care and neither does Everly apparently.

She's the one to break away, catching her breath and giving me what can only be described as bedroom eyes.

"I'll call you tomorrow," I say then open the door for her to enter through. If I don't then I'm likely going to pack her up and put her back in my car and head home. And she isn't ready for that yet. *Soon, though.*

"Thanks for today," Everly says then turns as she walks through the door a little wobbly and it makes my chest expand. "It was amazing."

"Only because you were there," I admit.

"Night."

"Sleep well, angel."

I watch her walk over to the elevator before I make my way over to the car where Dale is.

"To the office," I instruct him.

Going back to an empty home has no appeal and now that the entire Kevin Jenkins debacle came to light, I need to get caught up on some much-needed work.

Two weeks.

That's how long it's been since I've been able to spend any quality time with my angel. Two very long, very tiring weeks of late nights at the office.

I've been swamped with acquiring half of that asshole Kevin's workload.

"Your Honor, if it would please the court, I'd like to request an extension for the trial." I'm standing at the table with my client, Dustin Barker, and two other firm associates that I'm questioning as to why I hired them.

Olivia and I decided to split Kevin's caseload, instead of pushing it off onto the other busy associates. Apparently, Kevin was a go getter in obtaining cases. He had multiple trial court cases that were happening all at once. I guess he thought he could slide in those false reports, and they'd go unnoticed until the right time to implode my world.

"Your Honor, we've already been delayed twice now, and the people would like to move this along so that justice can be served," District Attorney Burt Buttons pipes up, interrupting what Judge Border was about to say. His nasally voice still irks me ten years later.

"Yes, we have. Mr. Thorne, what is the reasoning behind

another delay?" Judge Border questions as he pulls off his black rimmed glasses and tosses them in front of him.

"I'm," I pause quickly, almost admitting that I've lost my witnesses that Kevin had down. "There have been a few new developments that are crucial to my client's innocence. If we could just delay another few weeks—"

"Few weeks?" D.A. Buttons squeaks. "You've had over seven months to prepare for this Thorne."

I refuse to turn my head and sneer at the fat fuck in a cheap suit, who desperately needs hair plugs.

"Your Honor, this was one of my associates' cases and he is no longer with the firm. So, I'm asking for more time so that I'm able to fully prepare and be brought up to date."

"You have one week. That is all, one week Mr. Thorne. Both of you get with my secretary, Patty, for a time slot." He bangs the gavel, then stands to exit back into his chambers.

I sigh a huge relief. I've never had a case that is a clusterfuck of epic proportions before. I swear, if I were to run into Kevin, I think I'd beat the shit out of him right on the steps of the courthouse.

"Can't seem to find the rabbit to pull out of your magical hat on this can you, Thorne?" Button taunts.

There are some days I'd wished I'd gone into a different occupation, like boxing, especially when I have to deal with pompous assholes like him.

"I don't need a hat or rabbit when you've got a leak in your office," I volley to get under his skin. He doesn't have a leak but that doesn't mean I can't start trouble or put doubt between him and his workers. His face turns bright red with fury, and I can't help but smirk.

Gathering up my files, I decide to leave him with those parting words. I shake Dustin Barker's hand and tell him that I'll be in touch, then leave without so much as a word. I've got my work cut out for me and all I see are a lot of late nights at the office and black coffee in my future.

Dale parks the car at the curb of my office, and I see Olivia approaching. She looks just as worn out as me.

"Hard day in court?" I ask, holding open the door for her.

"You have no idea. Judge Spring was in a mood today. How'd yours go? Any better?"

"Not much but I did get another extension on the Barker case. That should give me enough time to tie up the rest of Kevin's cases, then focus solely on my own workload. I also found out that Buttons is the prosecutor on the Barker case and wasn't informed about it." All my associates know to let me know when the DA is handling the case. Kevin never let us know that Buttons was on the other side of the aisle and that makes me have even more questions as to what he was up to.

"Let me know if you need any help, I should be freed up over the next few days."

We exit off the elevator, then head our separate ways towards our own offices.

"Hello Mr. Thorne," Ruby, my secretary, greets as I walk towards her.

"Morning Ruby."

"Your next appointment just arrived. I told them to go ahead and wait in your office."

That's odd, Ruby knows to never let anyone in my office unless I'm already here. I've got a lot of sensitive information in there and in the wrong hands it could be bad. I nod, not wanting to snap at Ruby and run the risk of her putting laxatives in my coffee, then briskly walk the few feet to my office.

When I open the door, the lights are off, but soft music is

playing in the background and the smell of vanilla waifs in my nose. The same smell that reminds me of my woman. The blinds are even pulled down making it hard to see anything.

Maybe Ruby is more than ready to retire?

Flipping the switch, the lights shine and as my eyes adjust they track to the sexiest pair of fuck me heels propped up on my desk. They are attached to slender tan legs that lead to a pair of short black shorts. The woman is leaning back in my butter-soft leather chair. Her hazel eyes shine with mischief.

"You're late, Mr. Thorne." Her voice is soft yet commanding as she rises up from my chair and leans down, placing both hands on my desk.

If I didn't already have a fantasy of role playing here in my office, I do now.

"I apologize Ms. Bryant, court ran longer than expected," I counter and latch the lock to my door. I'm going to need a private meeting with this client.

"My time is very costly Mr. Thorne, so let's make sure this doesn't happen again, or else I'll be forced to look elsewhere for services." Her eyes dance with mirth and I can't help but chuckle as she makes her way around the desk.

Her white blouse has a few buttons undone, where I can peek at the tops of her full breast. She doesn't even know the storm brewing inside of me. We haven't seen each other in two weeks, except for a few video calls, and I'm like a man in the desert looking for something to quench his thirst.

My briefcase hits the floor with a thud as I stalk toward my prey. She's what I've been dying to see and have denied myself over the last two weeks because of work. *Never again.* I need to make her a priority above all else. The saying, *if you don't water your grass then someone else will,* comes to mind and my fist tightens at the thought of someone else stepping in and taking my spot with Everly.

"Missed you," I say as I crush her body to my chest. Even in heels, she's still quite a bit shorter than me.

"Missed you too."

Not wanting to wait another minute, I crush my lips to hers. Everly kisses me back with the same enthusiasm, almost climbing me like a tree. My hands grab the back of her thighs, and her legs automatically wrap around my waist. She weighs nothing, I could toss her around like a doll and not work up a sweat. After a while, we finally break apart and stare into each other's eyes. Talking on the phone for a few minutes and texting wasn't cutting it for me; I need this connection with her. I need the physical aspect of it with her, to have her present in my life.

"Thought you might need a session." She interrupts the silence and nods over to the portable table next to the window.

My heart actually starts to beat faster at the thought of her thinking about my well-being. When was the last time someone thought enough about me like this? I don't deserve this woman but I'm too selfish to walk away and lose the most important person in my life.

Walking over to the table with her in my arms, I place her ass down on the edge.

"Right now, I need to have my mouth on every inch of your delectable body," I tell her, pulling away. I start to undress, letting my clothes fall to the floor in a pile.

Her breath hitches and I watch her eyes roam over my naked chest, as I reach for my belt. I yank the belt out of the loops then unhook the button of my pants. Slowly, I bend down and pick up one of her legs with my hand as I release her tiny foot from her heel. My mouth presses to her ankle and I feel her moan all the way down to where our skin meets.

"Linc," she tilts her head back as she leans back on her elbows.

"Just lay there and let me take care of you," I tell her as I move up her calf. Her toned legs are a work of art and so soft.

As I work my way up her body, I reach her small black shorts. Her eyes meet mine and she gives me a nod, then lifts her hips off the table. My fingers skim up her hips, then start to pull the thin material down over her plump ass and legs. I lick my dry lips when a pair of microscopic panties barely cover her weeping pussy. There is a dark wet spot on the front where her body wants my attention.

"I'm going to make you feel so good, angel."

I reach down with my hands, placing them on the outside of her hips at the string and snap them apart, crumbling the lace off her skin. Smoothness stares back at me as I assess her mound that has a small thatch of hair at the top. My cock leaks at the sight and I reach down and adjust him in a more comfortable position.

Planting both hands on either side of her body, I hover over her, bringing our faces together.

"As much as my dick wants to claim your pussy right now, I'm not going to. The first time I have you, it'll be in my bed and where others can't hear the sounds that are only reserved for me," I tell her as her chest rapidly rises and falls. Her eyes match mine, filled with lust. "But I am going to drink all that sweetness pouring out of you."

My lips press against hers at the same time my fingers make contact with her pussy. She gasps and I slide my tongue in and sweep it against hers. She wraps her arms around my shoulders and her fingers coast up into my hair. My hips move involuntarily and bump into the apex of her thighs. I circle her channel and feel the pulse calling for more.

"Mmhmm," she groans at the sensation as I release my lips from hers and start to descend toward her neck leaving a wet trail to the top of her breasts.

"This won't do," I say at her covered torso. Pulling my hand away from her heat, I bring it up and start to make quick work removing the offending clothing. Once I have the white shirt off, I move to discard the matching bra. I release the catch and her ample breasts spill into my hands, causing me to groan. "Beautiful," I state looking at them as they fill up more than my hands.

Leaning down, I waste no time licking and sucking one into my mouth as I play with the other. Her nipples are hard as diamonds, and they are the perfect shade of pink. Everly's hips come off the table and skim against my cock looking for friction. I thrust up, bouncing her and letting her feel how hard she makes me, before switching to her other breast giving it the same attention as the first one. After a few minutes, Everly, who is now laid back flat on the massage table, unknowingly starts to press my head down to where her body wants all the attention. She's soaked the front of my pants, and I feel the head of my dick sticking out the top of my boxers.

"I'm going to devour this pussy until you drown me in your cum."

I move down, pressing more wet kisses, until I reach her slit. My tongue starts to stroke over her core, giving light taps against her clit.

"Linc, so good," she moans with every pass.

I rub my index finger around her tight hole and push gently in, breaching her wet cavity. I groan my pleasure when I feel how small and tight she is. I'm delighted the moment I come into contact with that treasured thin membrane of skin that my dick will have the honor of bursting through, I pull back not wanting to disturb that precious gem. She moves to adjust to the intrusion, so I capture her clit with my lips and suck to ease any discomfort. Her channel feels so good as I start to work my finger in and out, sucking and swirling my tongue to give her all the pleasure her body can take. I take my free hand and reach up, palming her tit and twisting her nipple, overloading her senses.

"Linc I'm coming," she pants with her head thrown back.

Her walls start to quiver around my finger and before I'm able to add another finger to loosen her up a little more, she floods my mouth with her juices. Her body takes over spasming, as I continue my assault in wringing all of her pleasure from her. I drink from like she's the fountain of youth, and don't stop until she's pushing me away. I've got her cum all over my mouth.

I stay on my knees at the end of the table and watch her as she comes down from the orgasm. Her beautiful smile enamors me every time.

"That felt so good," she says as she tries to lift her prone body up.

"You taste even better than I thought," I say as I stand up and press my mouth to hers, letting her get a taste of her own delicious orgasm.

The moment our lips touch, she's all over me. She wraps me up in her arms and my hands graze over her naked body. She places her hands against my chest and gives me a nudge. I move back slightly, not breaking our lips as we consume each other. Everly is the one to break our connection, as she looks right up at my eyes with so much fervor in her. I watch as she slides down onto the rug to her knees, never losing eye contact. I've jerked off to this so many times in the shower, imagining what she would look like. The fantasy is nothing compared to the real thing, as my cock thumps in beat with my heart.

"You don't have to do this, angel," I tell her cupping her cheek, not wanting her to feel pressured to return the favor.

She smirks, then brings her hands up to my zipper, drawing the metal down. She hooks both hands in and pulls down my pants and boxers as my hard, hot dick falls out, bouncing right in front of her face. I groan as her tongue juts out and swipes up a dribble of my cum. Everly extends her neck and wraps her plump lips around the head of my cock. The moment she touches him, he jumps in her mouth. Her warm, wet mouth has me feeling light-headed as I place a hand on the table to steady myself.

"Wrap your hand at the base, angel," I try not to sound too commanding, but she's got me so worked up.

She does as she's told, then starts to pump that hand as she tries to take more of me down her throat. I'm a big guy so I know, when she makes it halfway and gags, that she's going to need some practice to take all of me on her own. Once she finds her rhythm, my free hand finds its way into her hair, helping guide her to take more.

"That's it baby, take a few more in," I encourage as she dips down taking more. She hums and it goes straight to my sack. I've been on the edge of erupting since she put her mouth on me, and the vibration breaks my restraint. I'm starting to pant like a dog in heat as she picks up her pace. "I'm about to come baby. I want your eyes," I say out of breath.

The moment she looks up into mine, I see her smeared eyeliner but it's her eyes that capture me. My world clicks into place, and I know that this is all I'll ever want for the rest of my life. She licks the underside and sucks the head while pumping her hand on my rod, and I lose it. Cum bursts out of my dick, in long thick ropes. She gags as her mouth fills to the brim, but she swallows every drop. I eventually fall from her lips as she sets back on her heels, wiping the corners of her mouth while still keeping her eyes on me.

"I might need a nap after that," I say and help her up from the rug.

"This wasn't what I had in mind when I came here to relieve your tension," she says, picking up her clothes as I pull my boxers and pants up.

"I'm pretty sure I'm having my doctor write up a daily prescription for what you just offered. I think you missed your calling, angel."

She giggles as she buttons up her white shirt.

"Let's go have that nap, Casanova," she says as she's getting everything gathered up.

I watch her for a few seconds as I picture my life in the next few years. Every one of those years flash with her in it. And I know right then and there that I'd follow her anywhere.

CHAPTER NINE

"Knock, knock!" I hear from the door of the employee locker room. "You've got some visitors here to pick you up," Lisa, our receptionist, announces.

"Visitors? As in more than a handsome man in a suit?" I ask.

Linc and I are going to dinner with his parents and grandparents this evening. According to Linc, his grandma has been wanting to meet me for a while after she found out Linc and I were seeing each other.

"Yes, the cutest old couple I've ever seen said that they were here to pick you up."

My eyes widen, "I'll be right there."

I finish swiping my gloss across my bottom lip, then poof up my hair one last time in the mirror. Now I'm even more nervous. What if they don't like me? What if they think I'm not good enough to date or be with their grandson? I blow out a heavy breath, then gather up my bag that contains my work clothes and makeup. I wasn't going to have enough time to go home and change after work, since we were meeting his family for an early meal so I brought it with me.

Walking down the hall, I reach the foyer and see exactly what Lisa was talking about. Linc's grandparents are standing to one side of the front counter, with one of our brochures in hand, asking about all the services. Eleanor, his grandma, is wearing a patchwork button up shirt with a cute visor, that old people wear when gardening, along with a fanny pack around her waist. His grandpa, Archie, has on a pair of tall white socks, khaki shorts and a tucked in buttoned up collared shirt. His full head of gray hair is combed over, and he's wearing a pair of black rimmed glasses. All that's missing is a pocket protector in the front pocket of his shirt and he'd be the guy for a 1950's poster. They are adorable and my nervousness calms slightly. They don't seem like your typical rich snobby Hollywood elite, even though Linc has said that they are extremely well off.

"Hi, I'm Everly. You must be Eleanor and Archie," I greet as I come up next to them.

"Oh, honey look how beautiful she is," Eleanor states as she swats her husband to look up from the brochure. "She looks normal, and she eats!" My eyes grow double in size at her comments. "I'm Grandma," She introduces as she hugs me.

I embrace her and watch Archie chuckle when she pulls back from greeting me.

"She was worried you were going to be made more of plastic than natural beauty. I'm Archie, sweet girl, or Grandpa, whichever you're comfortable with." He pulls me in for the same hug and I can't help but already love them. They smell of home and are so genuine.

"I hate needles, so I don't think you have to worry about that with me," I tell them as we stand there in the lobby.

"You are much prettier than Linc told us," Eleanor says as she looks me over again. "And you have the perfect hips for birthing our great grandbabies."

"I—" she caught me off guard with her statement but I also love how blunt she is.

"Ellie, let's not scare her off just yet. Remember, Linc wants us to make a good first impression. And I thought you wanted to check out this spa before we head back out to Montana." Archie tries to rein in his wife, but she just waves him off. I can hear Lisa trying to hold in a laugh from behind the counter and I can't help but smile. I think I'm going to love them.

"Would you like a tour of the spa before we leave?" I ask.

"I'd love to see it," she states. "You stay here," she tells her husband as we make our way down the first hall that I occupy.

"What do you do here?"

"I'm a masseuse," I tell her.

"So, you're touching naked bodies all day?" She asks, scrunching up her face in distaste. "I'd hate to see all that flabby skin bouncing around."

"Their privates are always covered," I inform her, but my mind goes back to a very naked Linc and how not an inch of that man is flabby.

We walk down towards the sauna and the mineral pools, then back up to the treatment rooms where they do facials, and the medical procedures and injectables.

"I'm starving, let's go eat," Eleanor suggests, then grabs for my hand and starts walking toward the front door. Archie falls in line as we make our way outside.

When we get to the parking lot, a man in a black suit is waiting by a town car. When he sees us, he opens the back door.

"Lincoln doesn't trust us to drive around the city when we

come into town anymore," Eleanor says with a huff as the driver pulls out of the lot.

"That's because you almost started a riot on the freeway, dear," Archie shifts so he can look back from the front seat to look at us.

It makes me giggle and I see Eleanor cross her arms over her chest, getting ready to defend herself. Just when she opens her mouth, the driver pulls up to a popular restaurant for celebrities.

"Why the hell did we come to this place?" Eleanor snaps. "The last thing I want is to be photographed while stuffing my face."

The driver opens our door, and I slide out after Eleanor.

"Your son, or Alice, must've picked it," Archie comes up to her side and wraps his arm around her shoulders. "Let's just get through the meal, then I'll take you to get your favorite gelato." He tries to placate her, and I love how much they banter but also love each other. It's so rare to see couples stick it out for more than ten years nowadays.

As we stand near the curb, another car pulls up and Linc climbs gracefully out of the car. He smiles over at us, but flashes start to go off and we watch as a woman in a tight, almost see through dress, comes from the restaurant and towards the valet area.

"Linc!" the woman shouts, then waves, turning all our attention to her. She strides over and wraps her arms around his waist. The cameras are snapping away, and I watch as she poses, making comments and laughing as if Linc is saying the funniest thing.

Linc

I'm running late for dinner with my family, who are meeting Everly. When Grandma called earlier and heard that I was behind schedule, they offered to pick up her and bring her to the restaurant. I was reluctant at first, but I know that Grandma and Grandpa will make her feel like family. Dale, who raced across town from a meeting, pulls up to the valet. I hate coming to this restaurant, where you come to be seen and put in the media for a headline. I was hoping for a quiet place to sit down and not be interrupted, so that both my parents and grandparents could properly meet Everly.

As I get out, I see Everly and my grandparents walking up.

"Linc!" I hear my name being called, and when I turn my attention away from my woman I see Blaire.

Blaire and I have a complicated relationship. I took her on as a client when I first opened my firm. She and I have—or had—a mutually beneficial agreement where her modeling agency would supply me with dates to get my face and name out with the media and at functions and in return, I would give her a huge price cut in my fee. Over the years, as I became more well-known and famous, my clientele list became more elite and I continued to win all of my clients' cases. She and I would hook up a lot throughout the years and, at the time, I didn't mind but now that I have Everly, I want to make sure the two worlds don't collide.

"I've missed you, babe," she says as she wraps her arms around my waist, as the paparazzi's cameras click away.

My hands snag her wrist and gently remove her from touching me.

"*Lincoln, are you and Blaire together?*"

"*Lincoln, we saw Linley yesterday and she said that you and she were still together. Is that true?*"

"*Blaire, did you steal Lincoln away from Linley while she was in Europe?*"

I used to love the attention this brought, and would eat this moment up, but as I look over to where my grandparents and Everly are, I realize how much of an annoyance this is. The disgusting look on Everly's face shatters something in me.

I hear Blaire's obnoxious laugh, and it sounds like nails on a chalkboard. Ignoring her and the paparazzi, I make my way over to the group.

"Hey, angel, you look great," I greet Everly, wrapping my arms around her and then pressing my lips to hers. The sound of clicking has me pulling back, remembering we're out in public. I pull back, tucking her into my side and then turn toward my grandparents, ignoring the questions the paparazzi are asking ten feet away. "Thanks for picking her up." I lean in and give Grandma a kiss on the cheek and shake Grandpa's hand.

"It was no problem. Everly gave Ellie a tour of the spa," Grandpa says.

"Can we go in already? I'm tired of being stared at," Grandma states glaring down the paparazzi.

"Of course, Grandma," I motion for her and Grandpa to go ahead of us, then follow behind, as I put myself between me and the group of men gathering for a picture. "Sorry about all this. I didn't realize Mom booked this place until about thirty minutes ago. I'd preferred going somewhere less flashy."

"That's what Eleanor was saying," Everly giggles and it puts a smile on my face.

As we approach close to the door, Blaire is standing there staring at us. A frown mars her face.

"And who is this?" She asks.

As much as I want to escape into the restaurant, I also don't want to cause a scene, so I let my grandparents head in while I hold Everly and myself back.

"Blaire Hutchins, meet Everly, my girlfriend," I introduce.

"Your… girlfriend?" She sounds shocked at first, but then bursts out in a laugh like I just told her a joke. My back straightens as I lock Everly closer to me. Blaire must read the room because she abruptly stops laughing. "I didn't know you were seeing anyone, especially after our last *meeting* together."

I know what she's referring to and I refuse to acknowledge or make Everly feel uncomfortable.

"Ms. Hutchins is a client with the firm. She owns a modeling agency," I tell Everly.

"Oh, don't be so modest, Lincoln," Blaire says, reaching over and squeezing my upper arm. "I only sign the world's best models." She's giving me her best bedroom eyes look, and I can't help but feel uncomfortable, so I can only imagine what Everly must feel like.

"Are you guys coming to the table or should we eat without you?" Grandma's voice yells from the door, and I've never been more grateful.

"Have a nice evening," I tell Blaire, and before she can respond I'm ushering Everly around Blaire and through the door of the restaurant, following Grandma to our table towards the back.

My parents are already seated, and both stand as we approach.

"Sorry for running late," I greet Mom with a peck on the cheek and a handshake to Dad. "Mom, Dad this is Everly Bryant. Everly, this is my mom, Alice, and my dad, Daniel," I introduce.

"It's nice to meet you both," Everly shakes both of their hands and gives them a sweet smile. We take our seats with my woman sandwiched between me and Grandma.

"Whose idea was it to come here?" Grandma scrunches up her face while looking over the menu.

"I thought we could have a nice family meal while meeting Everly," Mom says defending her choice.

"We could've done that at the burger joint two streets over. At least we know the food is edible there," Grandma chides and I watch Grandpa smirk. Grandma tends to bluntly say what everyone else holds in.

I sit there and observe Everly, looking back and forth, as my mom and grandma continue to explain to each other their side as to why we should or shouldn't be here.

"So Everly, our son tells us you're a massage therapist," Dad interrupts the conversation between the two women after a waiter comes around to get our drink orders.

"Yes sir, for the past three years," she answers, and I reach over under the table and thread our fingers together.

"You didn't want to go to college?" Mom questions, as she takes a sip from her wine glass.

Everly smiles, "No, I didn't think college was for me. I had good grades in school, but I couldn't see myself going another four years with a degree I wouldn't use."

"And your parents agreed with your choice?" Dad asks.

"Dad—" I go to intervene because it's really none of his business why.

"I haven't had contact with my mother since I was nine. And my dad fully supports my career decision."

"I think it's wonderful not to go into debt for something you'd never use," Grandma pipes up. "Smart girl."

"Thank you, Eleanor," Everly sends a relieved nod towards her.

"Call me Grandma, dear."

The waiter comes back and takes our order for dinner as the table goes quiet. Mom and Grandma go back and forth over where to have the next family vacation. When the meal comes, we tuck in.

"How are things going in the Barker case?" Dad asks between bites.

"As good as can be expected," I say. I've told him about the instance with Kevin Jenkins and how he tried to sabotage me. He was floored that someone would go to such an extent.

"Let me know if you need a fresh pair of eyes."

"I will," I tell him, but I know I won't. Talking business with him is not something I strive to do after I left his firm and opened mine.

"You both have successful firms. Why did you split from each other?" Everly innocently asks, not knowing the landmine she just stepped on. There is an immediate unease at the table now as she notices that everyone won't make eye contact.

"My firm's specialty is mostly divorces whereas Lincoln decided it wasn't as glamorous, and left to have his face splashed all over the media." Dad really seems so bitter; he's not pulling any punches.

"Honey, let's not do this here, in public. I thought the two of you worked through this?" Mom tries to mediate the '*Great Debate*'.

"Oh, I'm so sorry. I didn't mean to—" Everly tries to apologize for something she didn't know was a hot button in our family.

I place a hand on her thigh, "It's okay, you didn't know but it's something that you should. I left Dad's firm because I wanted to venture out and do more than watch husbands and wives tear each other up for petty shit."

"That's not all we do, Lincoln and you know it," Dad defends, tightening his hand on his tumbler. "I told you why I switched and only take on certain types of cases. All those years, I thought making a name for myself outweighed what was morally right. I just don't want you to be years down the road, having the same issues I suffer with. You have no idea how I still struggle with certain cases."

I turn to Everly, "Dad used to specialize in the criminal defense area that I do now, but grew a conscience apparently."

"That's a low blow, son." Dad fumes, then addresses Everly. "I took on a case where my client was accused of killing a young woman in cold blood. From start to finish, it was a nightmare to handle, but I was the best, and wanted to make sure he was given a fair trial. The case took months in court, and we were able to prove that my client was being set up. The wrong place and time situation, but after the not guilty verdict, my client proceeded to congratulate my colleagues and I in helping him get away with the perfect crime. He then told us how he'd targeted the murder victim, and exactly how he did it. I was sick for weeks, realizing the poor young lady and her family would never get the justice she so deserved. I decided that I didn't want to be a part of that anymore and switched the firm in a different direction."

I could hear Everly's intake of breath. "Oh, that is so horrible. What happened to that client?"

"This was a long time ago, but last I heard the client ended up dead from drugs of some sort."

"So that's what you do now?" Everly turns her doe eyes toward me, and for the first time since I became an attorney, I feel embarrassed.

"Every person has the right to a fair trial, Everly. I have the ability to turn away potential clients, whom I don't feel I can represent. Not all of them are like the one that Dad just described," I defend, hoping she doesn't look at me differently because of who I take on and advocate for. She nods and then picks up her glass. "Criminal defense is just one branch of my firm; we handle a lot of business and contract law as well. We are just known for the criminal side because it sells papers."

"Well, I think that's enough shop talk," Grandma chimes in, and I couldn't be happier.

The rest of dinner is spent with Grandma talking about Montana, and all the things her and Grandpa do out on their little slice of heaven. Everly tells them all about her time up there and the adventures she and her friend, Saylor, had hiking and exploring the great outdoors, just a few towns away from my grandparent's place.

We decide to leave through the back, to avoid the paparazzi, and as we say our goodbyes to my parents and grandparents, Grandma can't stop hugging Everly.

"Now you promised to come see me in Montana, so I expect a visit very soon," she tells her.

"I promise," Everly says with a laugh.

"Well, give me your phone so we can keep in touch." Grandma holds her hand out and Everly complies as Grandpa shakes his head.

"I think your grandmother might disown you if things don't work out between the two of you," Grandpa says as we watch them interact.

"Grandma doesn't have to worry, Everly is my end goal."

"That's good because we love her." He pats my shoulder. "Let's get the other boys together before we leave. Ellie wants to cook for you and talk about great grandbabies," he says with a chuckle.

"That'll go over well with Reid and Levi," I snort. "Tell her to make her famous lasagna and not to mention the subject until after their stomachs are full."

"We need to go Archie, or we'll miss our gameshow!" Grandma yells, not even ten feet away. "And you promised some gelato."

"And that's my cue. Remember the old adage *happy wife happy life'."* He pulls me in for a tight hug. "Love you, Lincoln. Take care of that woman of yours."

"Love you too, Grandpa and I will."

He steps over to Everly and gives her the same hug, then ushers Grandma over to their driver, where he's holding the door open.

"I love your grandparents," Everly says as we wave and watch them pull away from the curb.

"They are pretty special." I wrap my arm around her as we walk over to where Dale is standing by our car. "Would you like some dessert?"

"Depends on what kind," she bounces her eyebrows as we settle in the backseat.

"You and I are on the same page, angel." I hover over her, catching her lips to mine. "Hope you don't mind being tired tomorrow because I plan on having my treat all night."

CHAPTER TEN

Linc

The last month has been both trying and life-affirming. All these years I thought I was living but really, I was walking through the motions of life. Everly has brought color to my black and white world with her bright smile and loving being. Just knowing her has increased my life expectancy.

These past few weeks have shown me that Everly is the one I want in my life. I know at what capacity, but I'll give her some time to warm up to the idea of forever before I spring that on her.

Right now, I'm sitting in the courtroom with my client Dustin Barker, waiting for the jury to return with their verdict. The case was a clusterfuck from the beginning with our ex-employee trying to sabotage the case to get me disbarred. I'm just thankful we were able to catch it in time, before things got out of hand.

The case has been a nightmare of epic proportions. I have no doubt that my client should get off on the charges, as proper protocol and the chain of evidence wasn't followed correctly, which makes DA Burt Button's case look like a slice of Swiss cheese.

There are too many holes in the case and not being able to use all their evidence, it looks as though the case isn't linked to Mr. Barker.

When I first became an attorney, I was drawn in by the money and flashy lifestyle it brought. With each big win came more notoriety across the nation, which then, in turn, brought more clients with more money and the cycle continued after that. Being young and having the world thrown at your feet is a lot. The zeros in my account were never enough, so I worked and worked until another zero was added and my face was splashed on every news media outlet from here to the east coast. I thrived on it. It was a high; better than any drug I could inhale.

Until her.

Until Everly.

It was like she woke a sleeping giant. The cars and money and having my picture taken seems so petty now. She doesn't give two shits about any of that. The only thing that she cares about is my time. To spend time together, connecting on such an intimate level that has nothing to do with sex.

Sex.

Now that is something that I'd never thought would be an afterthought. I've never been a saint and lord knows I am a man with needs, but it never seemed right, as most of our time is spent talking and learning something new about the other.

Two days ago, Everly pushed to move things further along. We've fooled around, but never crossed the line where I took that little ripe cherry between her legs. This case that I've been working on has consumed just about every minute of my day, and I didn't want to rush through her first time, it should be savored, and she should be worshiped. That's why I've been planning this for a week.

"Last chance to make a plea deal before your client rots in an eight-by-eight cell." DA Buttons leans over the side of the table and into my personal space, interrupting my thoughts of how I plan the weekend to play out.

I can't stand it when someone thinks they're intimidating you. Imposing their authority, trying to beat on their chest to see who has the bigger balls.

Newsflash, I do.

"The only deal we're prepared to make is how many zeros the city is going to give my client for his rights being violated during this circus you'd like to call a trial. I'm even betting that us trying our case in civil court is going to cost the city a shit-ton of money," I counter.

The DA is sweating it and from the perspiration forming on his forehead and the sweat rings that are bleeding through his suit jacket, he's not so sure that he's got it in the bag. I on the other hand, know we're getting a win. That's what I do. I win. End of story. That's why I get paid the big money, to manipulate the law to fit the way I want it to bend. Some might think I'm a low life for getting criminals off, but I don't see it that way. If the prosecution was good at his job and did things the correct way, then my client would be spending life in prison without the possibility of parole because the actual evidence would show he killed his girlfriend and her lover. The DA doesn't have a pot to piss in after I blew up every bit of evidence his detectives scoured. They botched up the entire case, hoping Mr. Barker was only going to stay with his court appointed attorney, who couldn't find his head from his asshole. Yeah, I'm the guy you call now if you need to get out of a bad situation.

Buttons narrows his eyes, once again going for the intimidation route, when a voice booms over the room.

"Court will resume in five minutes!"

Buttons straightens, turning towards the front of the courtroom.

"I guess we'll just have to take our chances," I jovially say, while shoving my phone in my jacket pocket and papers in my briefcase.

"One of these days you're not going to win, Thorne. One day you or that brother is going to lose, and it will be the most devastating thing you ever experience; not only to your ego but to your soul. A person can't win every time; sometimes a hard fall is just around the corner when we least expect it."

"But not today."

The DA shakes his head, then moves to the other side of the room to his table, as the judge comes in.

"All rise," the bailiff announces, and we all stand as the judge takes his seat in his black leather chair.

"The jury has reached a verdict so if the bailiff will please escort them in."

One by one the jurors come in and take their assigned seats in the jury box. None of them are attempting to look over in our direction, and for the first time I'm frozen. This could go two different ways. First, they could be avoiding looking over here because they're ashamed to be letting a guilty man go free. Or they're avoiding us because they decided he was guilty, and went against the judge's rules as to follow the letter of the law, and they decided to sweep it under the rug and send his ass to prison. I'm almost certain it's the first one but you never know, with some people, how they feel about getting their own justice instead of following the rules.

"Can the foreman please stand and recite the verdict that was written by the jury."

A man in his forties stands and begins the long dialogue of

the required reading. He states the long list of charges that my client is facing, and my lungs automatically squeeze tight. They do this with every verdict on every case I've ever done. My record is impeccable, but there will come a day when I do lose, so I silently hold my breath waiting in case today is that day.

Not guilty.

Not guilty.

Not guilty.

All three charges that Dustin Barker was facing, he has been found *not guilty*, and I release the breath I was holding. The courtroom bursts out in a commotion but there are several officers here to deal with that.

"After the results from the jury, Dustin Barker, you are free to go."

The gavel slams down and court is adjourned.

"You did it!" My client celebrates next to me and throws his arms around me.

Of course I did, that's what you paid for.

"Try to stay out of trouble from now on," I chide as I shake his hand, then do the same to my associates who worked overtime on this case.

"Sure will."

With that, he takes off to a group of people who were seated behind us in the courtroom, to celebrate. Chances are we'll be seeing him again as a client within the next two years, now that he's free. All idiots who think they're invincible usually do, which means charging even more the next time I have to bail his ass out. Job security is what my dad always said when I worked for his company the first year after law school.

"How can you live with yourself? You just got a man off on two counts of murder."

Once again DA Buttons is up my ass before I even make it to the door of the courtroom. He knows that when I step outside the media is going to be circling, because I've once again gotten another client off.

"Me? If you'd done *your* job then we wouldn't be sitting here in the first place. Had your people followed the law then it would've been an open and shut case. Don't blame me for your shortcomings. I did *my* job, what did you do?"

I push past him and out in the crowd of media yelling to get their questions answered. My client is beside me as I go through all the ways Burt Buttons is nothing but a fuck up and the people suffer under his leadership.

Two hours later, I'm dropped off at the office as everyone congratulates me on another notch to add to the wall of wins. *Yeah, yeah, I'm good.*

"Mr. Thorne, I've had several calls from news outlets, wanting an interview with you or Mr. Barker," Ruby, my secretary tells me as I pass her desk.

"Send them to PR and have them set something up after looking over my schedule for next week. I've told our client to lay low over the next few days, due to the backlash. I've sent over security to his hotel to monitor the situation." I pause just as I'm about to cross over into my office. "Can you set up for Dale to have the car ready half past five?"

"Of course, Mr. Thorne."

My phone dings and as I glance over at it, I can't help the smile. Why does hearing from her have me happier than my win today in court?

Everly: Just saw the news, congratulations on a big win!

> Me: Thanks, had it in the bag the entire time. Can you be here by 5:30? 😊 I've got plans for us tonight.

> Everly: If I rush. I'm covering for an employee in the morning, who has a sick kid. Hope that doesn't throw a wrench in things.

Shit, I was hoping to have her all to myself this weekend.

> Me: No worries, we'll work around it.

> Everly: Great! See you soon.

The rest of the day passes slowly. A knock on my door has me pulling my eyes from some documents.

"Got a minute?" Levi asks.

I toss my papers and pen on the desk and lean back.

"For you? Always," I say, giving him my full attention.

He comes in and heads straight over to the windows to look out. He has the same view, but this is where he always likes to stand when he comes in to talk with me.

"Congrats on the win today," he offers, but there is something in his voice.

"Thanks. What's going on bub?" I ask.

"Do you ever wish you picked a different career path and not the one we have?"

I have thought about it, especially when I left dad's firm to start this.

"Of course, but I can't really see myself as anything else." He turns to look over at me. "Are you wanting a change?"

"No… maybe. I don't know," he says, shaking his head.

"What's going on?" I ask and watch as his shoulders slump.

I've always felt as though Levi was my responsibility. Growing up after our parents died, it was me who made sure he was eating and bathing. When we moved from Washington to California, to live with Daniel and Alice, I was the one who made sure he did his homework and learned how to ride a bike. I'd taught him how to wash clothes and took on everything he needed. At first it was because I didn't know these people and the last thing I wanted was for a stranger to take advantage of him. As time went on it was just easier for me to make sure that he was taken care of. We were all I had left and I didn't want him to ever feel abandoned like I had when our parents left us. As the years went by we relaxed more around our new family and we let them in. I was thrilled that he wanted to follow in my footsteps going to Yale and then law school, but I could tell that he never really had that drive in him. Levi has always been the type of kid and adult who loves to work with his hands and be outdoors. Even now, I know that suit is making him itch.

"Do you think it's too late in life to make huge changes?"

"I guess it would depend on what you're wanting to change. Are we talking about moving somewhere else? Maybe a different specialty in the cases you're taking on, or not being an attorney at all?"

He looks back out the window, "All the above, maybe?"

The hair on the back of my neck rise. The only time I've ever been separated from my brother was when I was at college. Even then, I came home to see him all the time. We spoke multiple times a day. I feel like I'm really more of his parent, rather than a brother sometimes.

"Talk to me bub," I say, needing to know what he's feeling. The urge to fix whatever he's going through right now is strong, and I feel my heart hammering against my chest.

"I've just felt like I need a change recently. I thought I was happy here—"

"But?"

He shrugs and makes his way over to the chair across from me.

"Why don't you take some time off and go explore some things. Have one of the newer associates take over your workload then go out to Grandma and Grandpa's place. You love to hike out there and help repair their house. Get out of the city to clear your head. When you come back, we can sit down and look over everything. If you want a different career, then let's make that happen. I'll support whatever it is you want to do."

"You don't think it'll upset Dad?"

"I think you should do what is best for you and not what Dad or I think," I say whole heartedly. "I know I've encouraged you to follow me in my endeavors, but you should be doing what makes you happy. Not what others want for you."

Levi goes to stand, straightening out his suit.

"I'll think about it." He leaves without another word, and the last twenty years play over in my head. I wonder if I ever pushed him too much, or if I let my goals and ambitions be pressed on him. I've only ever wanted him to be happy and never feel the way I did when our biological parents died. Levi has such a soft soul that I worry some of the pressures of being an attorney have ruined him.

The phone on my desk buzzes, bringing me out of my thoughts. Ruby reminds me to file a document before the end of the day and I shift my focus back on work. I'll let Levi have some space for a beat then I'll circle back, and he and I can go for a beer and talk some more.

I spend the rest of the day working hard to make sure the rest of the weekend is cleared, and that I'm not interrupted at all, because I plan to spend it holed up in my penthouse with Everly. I've asked Tina, my cook and housekeeper, to stock the house with food and beverages. I also gave her a list to have done before she leaves for the weekend. She is a godsend after a long day at work; coming home to a homemade meal and a clean house is exactly what I need when things here don't go as planned. Also, I'm not the tidiest person in the world.

Just as I'm finishing up on some transcripts of another case that a very wealthy and influential client has called and begged for my help with, a knock interrupts my concentration. Before I can even call out to come in, the door opens and my angel walks in like she owns the place. At this point, she could ask for it and I'd sign it right over to her in a heartbeat.

"Hey handsome," she greets me as she walks around my desk with that sway in her hips that makes me groan every time I zone in on those curves. Everly plants a soft, quick kiss to my cheek and before I can reach out and grab those luscious hips, she pulls out of reach and rests on the end of my desk.

Oh, the memories we could make on this desk.

She's wearing a short off the shoulder dark teal dress, matched with silver heels. Her hair is curled and styled over her exposed right shoulder. Edible, that's what she looks like, and I plan on devouring her all night long.

"Hello gorgeous," I say, making a show of looking her up and down. Her firm trimmed legs are out for me to stare at and I can only picture what they're going to look like around my waist. "Ready to get some dinner?"

"Only if you are." Everly eyes me with a half hooded lustful gaze, and I almost clear my entire desk and lay her out on it. She's playing a very dangerous game with me and if I wasn't someone who prided themselves in total control then I'd do just that.

Pushing away from my desk, I quickly adjust my dick then grab for my suit jacket on the back of my chair. I plan to wine and dine her tonight and if I don't get out of this office, we'll never make it out of here.

"After you, angel." I gesture towards the door and once I see her hips sway away from me, I know I'm going to be a walking hard-on all night. *Maybe we should eat at the penthouse so no other fuckers can see her like this.*

"Have a great weekend, Ms. Ruby," Everly sweetly says to my secretary. They seem to get along well together ever since they first met over a month ago.

"Goodnight Ruby, have a wonderful weekend," I say in passing as I reach for Everly, making sure to tuck her into my side.

"Have a nice evening you two," she cheerfully says to us both. She already has her orders not to call this weekend, and I hope for her job's sake she passes off everything to Olivia if there's a major ordeal on our hands.

As the elevator doors open, Olivia pops out with a stack of papers in her hand. She finally looks up and sees me.

"Oh, good I was just coming to see you," she states looking back down at the documents.

"It'll have to wait until Monday," I tell her and move us around and step into the box.

"Monday?" she questions then looks up. "Oh, hi Everly, sorry I was distracted."

"Hey Olivia," my angel greets.

"I'm off until Monday and not to be disturbed," I tell her, giving her a pointed look.

"Really?" She raises an eyebrow, looking at me like I'm crazy.

"Really," I say deadpan. "I told Ruby to route any emergencies to you." I wink as she purses her lip together.

The doors close and I can't help the chuckle that leaves me at her shocked face. I rarely take any time off, so I know I'm throwing her for a loop.

"If you need to do some work, I'm okay to wait," Everly offers, and it makes me adore her even more. She's so understanding that sometimes I wonder if she truly is real. Most of the females I've experienced want all the attention and throw a fit to be the central focus.

"You are my priority this weekend. We are overdue to have some much-needed quality time together, without all the interruptions."

Dale is standing at the curb with the back door opened to our black sedan for the evening.

"Evening Mr. Thorne, Ms. Bryant," Dale greets us and helps Everly in the car.

"Everything all set for tonight?" I ask as I walk around the car to enter on the other side.

"Yes sir, everything is set according to Tina, and the restaurant has your reservation confirmed and is waiting for your arrival."

"Good."

"Where are we going to eat?" Everly asks, the excitement in her voice makes me feel like a kid again. Being around her is like experiencing everything for the first time. I forget that she's not used to the fancier things that I've lived with since my parents adopted me as a kid.

"Have you heard of Osteria Mozza?" She shakes her head. "It's an amazing Italian restaurant."

"I love Italian." She wrinkles her nose for a second. "You know I'd be happy with anything, right? We don't always have to go with something expensive and over the top."

"I know but I want my girl to eat the best." Everly blushes, then moves her eyes to our joined hands. "Plus, I want to make tonight special."

We spend the rest of the time talking about the verdict of my case that I won today. Everly tells me about some of the clients she had today, and I want more than anything to tell her she can't have male clients anymore but refrain. I know that'll be a battle I won't win, especially if she tries to say I can't have female clients as well. I trust her implicitly but it's the male population that I don't trust. Just one look at her and I was thinking about doing the dirtiest things to that sweet body. I can only imagine what others think about when she's massaging them.

As we pull up to Osteria Mozza, paparazzi are everywhere. Someone famous must be dining here too. When we exit the car, with Dale's help, we're bombarded with flashing lights and questions before we can make it to the entrance.

"Mr. Thorne, how does it feel to have another win under your belt?"

"Mr. Thorne, is your date the next up and coming model?"

"Mr. Thorne, how does Linley Lewis feel about your new female companion?"

I ignore them all, hoping Dale can navigate through the mob as I keep a death grip on her shoulder and try to shield her from all the lights. *Why the fuck do they keep bringing Linley up?*

"Mr. Thorne, we're sorry for the inconvenience. We had two professional athletes come in about ten minutes ago," the hostess says and immediately moves us to the other side of the restaurant, away from prying eyes and unwanted flashing lights.

As we pass other diners, my eyes lock on the two athletes who must've caused the mob outside. Both of whom are my clients, and who've been in trouble on several occasions, that I've had to pull their asses out of.

"Lincoln Thorne, good to see you man." Justin Taft, the short-stop of LA's MLB baseball team says, and stands to greet me.

"Justin," I say, shaking his hand. "It's good that I haven't seen you in a while."

He laughs as Kirk Captains, the first baseman, stands to do the same.

"And who's the little lady?" Kirk says homing in on Everly, who looks starstruck.

Damnit.

Laying claim to Everly, I place my arm possessively around her waist and squeeze her to my side.

"This is my girlfriend, Everly."

Kirk lifts an eyebrow, then nods his understanding. These ball players have no shame in hooking women. It's a different girl every night of the week, even on the road. I'll ruin Kirk if he even tries to make a move on Everly.

"Nice to meet you, Everly. What's a beautiful woman like you doing with a workaholic like this guy?" He jokes and much to my dismay, Everly laughs as they shake hands.

"I guess I have a sweet spot for dedicated men then. Linc is the best man I've ever met." She looks up at me and gives me the dreamiest eyes. Her statement makes me want to beat on my chest like a gorilla, then roar like a lion.

"We'll let you get back to your date. It was nice to see you again Lincoln, call us sometime and we'll go golfing or something," Justin says and lets us pass.

When we reach our table, I pull out Everly's chair but before she sits, she gives me a peck on the lips. I didn't know I was wound up until she pressed her lips to mine; that calmed my body immediately. She has the effect on me where she drives me wild but can turn around and soothe me.

We're given the menu, as our waiter was already at our table waiting before we sat down.

"Welcome to Osteria Mozza, my name is Anthony and I'll be serving you tonight. What drinks can I start you both out with?"

This place is amazing but when I look over, I can see Everly struggling with the menu.

She leans over and whispers, "Please pick whatever you want, I don't even know where to begin at a place like this."

I reach over and take the menu from her hands and give it to Anthony. I've been with Everly long enough to select food that I know she'll love.

"Don't worry I'll make sure you love every bite."

I tell the waiter our drink selection, then our order for the meal. I choose several dishes because I want Everly to try each one.

"We'll get this order out to you as soon as we can," Anthony says, then retreats towards the kitchen.

"Thank you." Everly shifts in her seat.

"You don't have to thank me. I'd do anything for you." My hand reaches over the white tablecloth and finds hers twisting around the stem of her water glass. She's nervous but I plan to make this as comfortable as possible.

Dinner was amazing but I think it had everything to do with the company I was keeping. We're on our way to my penthouse and a sense of nerves has taken up residence in my belly. Any other time I might think something was wrong with the food I ate but I know it's what's coming next that has me wanting to jump out of the moving car.

"Everything okay?" Everly asks, placing her soft, dainty hand over mine as Dale turns into the parking garage of my building.

Why does this feel like I'm the virgin here? Get a grip Thorne before she asks about my man card.

"Never better, angel." I kiss her knuckles as Dale opens her door and helps her out.

We walk to the elevator hand in hand, and I notice that her palms feel slightly damp. She's just as nervous as I am.

"We don't have to do anything you're not comfortable with."

Everly lets off a nervous laugh, something I've learned over the last few weeks she does to try to alleviate the tension.

The elevator reaches the top and opens to my door, without thinking I bend down and scoop her up in my arms.

"Ah! What are you doing Linc?" She squeals and locks her arms around my neck. Her smile is back and that was exactly what I was aiming for.

"I thought I'd carry you over the threshold." I playfully bounce her weightless body.

"That's for married couples," she says, and I stop in the middle of the doorway.

Married couples? I've thought a lot about marriage ever since meeting this angel, and it sounds natural when I think of the two of us.

"I think that has a nice ring to it, don't you?"

"What?" Her eyes widen. "Linc, we just met. Don't you think it's a little soon to be talking about this subject?"

"It's never too soon for that topic, but if you wish we'll shelve this discussion for future negotiations." Everly seems to relax, and I make a mental note to push the topic after I've got her naked and in a sex coma. She won't be able to put up a fuss after an earth-shattering orgasm. I wonder if she ever thought of a Vegas wedding. If she agreed, I'd waste no time in flying us over there and getting hitched tonight if that meant tying her to me for the rest of my life. Coming home every night to her beautiful face would be a nice change, instead of an empty apartment.

"Linc," she groans.

I walk us in and see that Tina has outdone herself. The place looks amazing, as vases of roses cover the apartment. Candles are lit and they lead towards my bedroom. The room where I plan on making Everly all mine, body and soul. I really want to tell her how I feel tonight, and I just hope she's at the same point in our relationship as I am.

"This is beautiful, did you do all this?" Everly asks as she takes in her surroundings.

"I had Tina set it up, but I told her what I was wanting," I admit and kiss her hairline. I still haven't placed her down on her feet because I don't want to lose this connection we've got going on right now. I feel like we're one when we're touching, and that is something I've never felt with another person.

The walk down the hall to the bedroom is just as decorated as the rest of the place. When I open the door, we're met with the same candles, roses and petals all over the room, letting off a floral scent. Everly lets out a giggle and I can't help but be concerned that I've overdone tonight.

"You don't like it?" I hesitantly ask.

"No, that's not it at all, but I can't help but think that the fire alarm is about to go off with all the candles burning."

She's right and the last thing I want is any interruptions for the rest of the evening.

"You're right. How about you blow out some of the ones in here while I take care of the living room."

"Deal." Her smile alone could light up a dark room and I love it.

I love her.

Gently, I set her on her feet, then whirl around to hurry and blow out all the flames. Man, how long did it take for Tina to light all of these? I wonder as I make my way from each one; there has to be at least a hundred.

Once I've made sure each one is out and not going to burn us down, I make my way back to the bedroom. This isn't the first time I've had Everly in my bed but it's the first time that we'll be making love, so I give myself a good pep talk before entering the room. She's standing at the end of the bed, and I can't help but watch her like a stalker.

"All done?" Everly asks as I stand against the door frame. She's blown out all but the last candle on the nightstand.

"Yeah," I say and glide across the floor until I reach her.

"Did you change the bedding in here or am I imagining things?" She points to bed, and I love how observant she is.

I did change the bedding and the sheets, along with the mattress and pillows. The things I did before and the people who were before her don't belong in the same room as Everly. I wanted to make sure I had a clean slate when I brought Everly to bed for our first time. I also changed the color of the paint on the walls. After being in her apartment and seeing how cozy she had everything decorated, I wanted my space I shared with her to have the same feeling. No longer does the room have a cold and sterile feel, but now it has a warm and inviting vibe to it.

"I did," I admit. "I want this to be a fresh new start for the both of us and our relationship."

She dips her head slightly, but my lips catch hers before she's able to turn from me. As soon as our lips touch, she melts into me, her body leans in and I waste no time in wrapping my arms around her waist, pulling her into me. Our tongues dance in synchrony as I taste the wine from the restaurant. Everly wraps her arms around my neck, making her body even closer to mine, with just a few thin pieces of material separating us from being connected in the most intimate way.

Slowly, I disconnect our bodies and kneel down at her feet.

"You are so beautiful," I say as I turn my eyes from her to her shoes.

Methodically, I release her tiny feet from the confines of her shoes, and my hands caress the soft, silky skin up her calf. Getting up from my knees, I swiftly move around to her back and plant the softest kiss to her exposed skin at her shoulders.

"I've dreamed of this moment from the first time I saw you at the courthouse," I whisper in her ear and receive a low moan as I nip at her lobe.

My fingers catch at the top of her dress, and I ever so slowly pull the zipper down to the top of her ass. Everly's breath has become more rapid, and I know that she's worked herself up waiting for my next touch, but I make her wait a bit longer. Wanting to feel my skin touching hers, I quickly lose my suit jacket and work the buttons to my shirt. As soon as the shirt hits the floor, my chest is caressing her exposed back.

"Linc," She pants as my fingers slide her dress down her shoulders and pools at her feet, next to her silver heels. Everly is left in only her white lace strapless bra and a matching white lace thong. The color is another reminder that she's going to give me the most precious gift a woman can give her man.

"I've never seen a person more perfect than you, angel. I'm one lucky motherfucker, baby and I plan to show you just what you mean to me."

Everly slowly turns and her breasts are barely contained in her bra. As my hands work to unhook the lace bra, my mouth moves to her kissable lips. After almost ripping the lace in two to get it off, I back away to get a real look at my perfect woman. The only item left is her panties which I'll rectify in a moment. Right now, I want to stare at the goddess before me.

A blush lightly appears on her cheeks, and it flows down towards the tops of her breasts. Not wanting her to cover herself, I start unhooking my belt and strip in front of her. I work hard for this body so I want to watch her eyes as I undress for her.

They don't disappoint as they watch my every move. As soon as I drop my pants, her body leans towards me. As if our bodies are magnets, forcing us to connect to one another. I kick my shoes and then socks off, leaving me in only my boxers.

"Do you like what you see?" I ask as the space between us is getting smaller and smaller.

She nods and reaches out for my boxers, and I let her take the lead for now.

"I'm nervous it's going to hurt," Everly whispers. Her hands are clenched to my waistband, but her eyes are lost in mine.

"I'd never hurt you, Everly. I've waited my whole life for you."

With my hands over hers, I help her pull the boxers down and off, piled with the other discarded clothing. Carefully, I lead her backwards to the edge of bed and lay her down. I'm a big boy and if I don't do some prep work, I'll split her in half. The last thing I'd ever want is to hurt her and make this a horrible experience for her.

Everly uses her hands every day to work on people to make them feel better and ease the aches for so many. I think it's my turn to make sure she's taken care of.

With my fingertips, I lightly work the soft skin and muscle

of her calf, then ease my way up her thigh. Her breathing is coming out in huffs of anticipation, and I haven't even touched her where she needs me the most.

"Do you like that, angel?" I ask, but already know my answer from the wet spot on the center of her panties.

I'm rewarded with a low moan, then a sharp nod.

Just as my fingers get close to her center, I release my hands from her body.

"Ah!" Everly grunts in frustration, and I can't help the smirk as I press a small kiss to her other ankle.

"Patience, angel," I murmur and work my nimble fingers up the second leg. One thing we've learned when we've been messing around this last month is that Everly is not a patient person when it comes to her orgasms.

Once I've thoroughly massaged all the way up her thigh, she is fisting the comforter. I've punished us both by taking this slow, but I want this to be a night we both remember until we're old and gray.

Leaning down, I kiss her belly button and nibble down to her panty covered center. Inhaling, I take in her sweet smell.

"I can't wait to be inside of you."

"Me either," Everly groans as I ever so slowly work her panties down her legs and sling them somewhere on the floor.

"I know you want my dick right now but if I don't get you ready, I'll hurt you and that's the last thing I'd ever want."

"Just do it," she impatiently moans.

Ignoring her pleas, I dive right in on her wet and wanting pussy. She's soaking for me and my cock grows even more than I thought possible. Her sweet juices ignite a fire within me, when it touches my tongue, and I feel like a starving man at a buffet. Her clit is enlarged and pulsing, as I eat her. She's not going to last long, so I take a finger and slip it in her channel. She's tighter than hell and writhing under my assault.

"Linc," she moans, and it makes cum leak from the tip of my cock. I love hearing my name on her lips.

"That's it, angel. Feel me."

I add a second digit in her warm, slick center and start a scissor motion to try to open her a little more. She's got the tightest pussy I've ever encountered, and I'm not sure how I'll fit inside her without it hurting. I feel her hymen right where I've left it but don't push any further. My dick gets the honor of breaking through it for his patience over the last month.

Everly's walls start to contract the more I rub against her hot tunnel, and I know she's about to come. We've done oral many times over the last month but for some reason it feels like our first. Her fingers grip my short locks as she pushes my face in further to her pussy, right as her legs stiffen.

"Linc!" she shouts as she pulses and her liquid gold gushes into my waiting mouth. I don't think I'll ever get enough of this woman laying here in my bed.

I want so badly to tell her my feelings for her but I'm afraid that what I'd say would scare the shit out of her. I know that I wouldn't stop at just saying the words but would actually haul her to a private jet and tie her to me forever. When I profess my love to her, I want her undivided attention, so she knows how much she means to me and that I'm all in.

Her body has little aftershocks from the orgasm, but I keep pumping my fingers to open her a little more. Everly's hooded eyes open and land on mine, as I sit up on my hind legs.

"I still can't get over how amazing it feels to have an orgasm that's not self-started." Her smile makes me feel like the tallest man in the world.

"You should expect more of those all weekend," I say then pull my fingers from her pussy and lick them clean. "Are you ready, angel? We don't have to go any farther if you don't want to," I say, giving her a chance to back out if she's still not ready, but I pray to God that she wants to keep going.

"If you wait any longer, I might combust." She groans and lifts up to pull me down so our chests are touching. Everly kisses me deep and I can't help but reciprocate as my cock has a mind of its own and lines right up to her lower lips.

Everly's legs go around my hips and the head of my throbbing cock starts to kiss her pussy lips. She's slippery and he decides it's time to get this party started.

"Ready?" I pull back and look into her perfect, trusting eyes.

She nods and my heart thumps a little faster in my chest.

"It'll hurt at first but then it'll be fine," I tell her as I see a little nervousness flash over her face.

We've talked about not using a condom and I went and got tested before we started messing around. I'd never forgive myself if I ever gave her something because of a stupid choice I made before she came along and changed my world. Everly's been on birth control for a few years and is pretty regular with her cycles. Although, I'd love nothing more than to tie her to me with a baby. I've never even thought about kids or marriage before this woman and she's making me rethink all my life-long decisions.

My dick inches in and her body goes rigid. She's squeezing me so tight I'm not sure I'll be able to fit all the way in at this point. I know I wanted to ease her into this but I'm starting to think the best way to get through this is by driving right in. After a few more moments, I decide that it is the only way to go.

"Okay, angel?" She nods but her eyes are closed. "Look at me," I tell her, and she complies.

Leaning down, I kiss the shit out of her and feel her relax just a bit; just like I was hoping. With her mind on the kiss, I thrust all the way and hold as I tear through her virginity and plant myself all the way to her womb.

"God you're tight!" I clench my teeth and hold my breath, pulling away from her lips. She whimpers and I hate there's nothing I can do right at this moment.

Quickly, I reach my thumb down to her clit and start circling. I know she's in a bit of pain and this is the only thing I can think of to ease her out of it. Our lips are pressed together again but they're not moving. She's holding her breath and she has her eyes closed tight. I hate that this is hurting her but in a way it feels good that I'm the one she's going through it with. I want all her firsts.

"You doing okay, angel?" I ask and slowly her muscles start to relax as she starts to breathe through her nose.

Her eyes finally open and I can tell she's holding back tears. Everly nods, "Yeah, I think so." Her voice trembles slightly.

"I'm gonna start moving, tell me if you want me to stop."

With slow and shallow thrusts, I start to move. She feels exquisite as my cock glides in and out of her wet channel.

"You feel so good. So warm and tight Everly. This pussy was made just for me, only me." She hums in response, and I keep going as my thrusts are coming quicker and the sound of our moans is all you hear throughout the room. Her pussy tightens even more around my dick, and I know she's getting close to another orgasm. Her body is now more relaxed and she's starting to move with me, with every pass.

"Oh, Linc it feels so good." Her nails dig into the flesh on my back and I welcome the pain.

I want to tell her that I love her and never want to let her go.

That she means everything to me and that I don't want to waste any more time apart. I want to come home every night to her here at our home. That she's opened this door I never knew was possible, and how we should jump in the deep end of the ocean without another thought.

But I don't. I don't tell her any of that but instead try and show her what she means to me. I caress her head and kiss every inch my lips can reach of her soft delicate skin.

"That's it angel, come for me. Feel that perfect pussy on my dick and cream me." She loves when I talk dirty when she's about to come.

Leaning down, my hips speed up even more as I feel my heavy balls start to draw up, ready for a release.

"It's coming—Linc I'm coming!" Her body tenses and her nails score my back as she comes hard on my dick. Her pussy contracts and I swear to all that is holy it feels like it could snap my shaft off. This pussy holds me like a vice, causing a tingle up my spine, and my dick grows a little thicker before a surge of cum shoots out of me and coats her insides. I feel like dynamite has just exploded in front of my eyes, as I unload every drop. After a few moments, my hips continue thrusting, even though I've got nothing left because she feels so damn good.

Finally, my body drops slightly forward as if all the life has been sucked out of me, but I manage to catch most of my weight on my forearms so as not to crush Everly.

Could this be hands down the best sex I've ever had? Hell yes it is!

When I finally regain the strength to open my eyes, I'm met with the most beautiful hazel eyes staring back at me. She's got the biggest smile on her face, and all my worries of hurting her fly out the window.

"Hey," I greet, matching her smile and then lean in to capture her lips with mine.

"Hey."

After everything we just did, Everly's cheek turns a dusty rose shade as her shyness creeps in.

"You okay?" I question, still connected with her. I refuse to move until she wants to.

"It was everything I had hoped it would be."

"Good because we'll be doing a lot of that from now on." I can't stop grinning and I'm afraid she's going to take me for a pussy if I don't get myself under control. "Are you hurting?" I move slightly to adjust my weight, and watch her flinch.

"More like stinging, I guess."

Carefully, I slide out of her and sit back on my haunches. The sight before me makes me want to worship her body all over again. Her pussy leaks our combined cum and my dick is covered in it too, along with a hint of her virginity.

"Wait right here," I say as I walk to the bathroom and turn the water to the tub on. When I have it at the perfect temperature, I walk over to the cabinet and grab a washcloth, bringing it over to the sink to wet. Walking back into the bedroom, I take this time to catalogue every little detail of this beautiful woman that is now mine. I'm still not sure how I got so lucky, but I'll never question my good fortune.

Taking the washcloth, I slowly place it over her pussy and let the warmth of the rag soothe the area.

"That feels good," she moans with a smile.

"Let's get you in the bath for a bit to ease the soreness," I say and reach down for her hand. She follows behind me at a slow pace, and I have to wonder if it hurts to walk. The asshole in me is proud to be the one to cause it.

We settle in the warm water with her back to my chest, and the weight of her against me loosens a knot in my chest. She's what I've been waiting for my entire life, and I can't wait to tell her. Tomorrow after she gets out of work, I've got another evening planned out and that's when I'll spill my soul and confess to her what she means to me.

CHAPTER ELEVEN

Everly

I'm on cloud nine as I walk through the back doors of work.
Everything looks so much more vivid, as if my eyes are opening for the first time in my life. It's like I'm taking the time to
stop and smell the roses. Last night was everything I'd hoped it
would be. And more!

Linc was great at being patient and gentle, making sure I was
ready. He did things to me that I'm not even sure most of those
erotica books I've read have in them. My nerves were getting the
best of me, but Linc squashed them with a single touch or kiss,
making me believe that there are true men out in the world.

"Someone had an amazing night," Lisa, our receptionist, announces to the lobby.

I'm sure my blush is giving everything away. I wanted to call
Saylor this morning and spill the beans, but she was meeting her
mysterious man from the bar again. When I've pressed her about
him, all she told me was that she'd tell me after this weekend.
She's been avoiding me like the plague so I know something is
up with her.

"How's my schedule look today?" I ask, avoiding her gaze as she stares at me to blab the details.

"Girl, you're going to have to do better than that," Lisa says a little too loud, making even more noise and gaining attention from people passing by the desk. "You're practically floating across the floor and that grin tattooed on your face says it all."

After not commenting for a few long moments, holding my ground, Lisa finally gives in and starts tapping away on the computer.

"Fine, but I expect details after work or I'm going to put Mr. Sasquatch on your regular rotation," Lisa playfully threatens.

We have an older man in his late seventies who schedules an appointment every Tuesday afternoon. I think his real name is Todd or Bob, but he's covered in hair like it's a second shirt. He always has the foulest odor and thinks all the girls want him. He flashes his money like it's gum trying to impress anyone who's watching. He looks like bigfoot in a way, so the name stuck. Lisa has the honorary duty of placing him on the schedule for all the massage therapists and gives him to the girls she's hating on at the moment. Which is why I always try to bring her some of Saylor's baked goods to butter her up.

"Okay, okay. I'll tell you a smidge of why I'm so happy," I say to her and she all but shushes the lobby to listen in. "...after work."

"You're a real buzz kill, Everly, but I love you, so I'll let it slide this time."

"Thank you," I say even though I'm not sure why. I love working here and all of us get along so well together.

"You've got a new client in thirty minutes. She's wanting to release some tension. She looks familiar but who knows, and then you're booked with Cammie's regulars every hour until five, with an hour lunch at one. Cammie called and wanted to say thank you once again for taking on her clients today and that her daughter is doing better."

She prints up my list and I make my way towards the massage wing of the building to treatment room nine.

"I'm sticking around until you're done so don't think you can sneak away without talking with me!" Lisa shouts across the room and I pick up my pace to get away from her. She really is a fun girl when she lets her guard down.

I'm in my room making sure everything is stocked up for my new client, when there's a knock on the door and Saylor steps in. I haven't turned on the light letting others know I'm in session yet. She's got a box in her hands, and I can smell the fresh croissants from across the room, making my stomach grumble. Every Saturday, she brings pastries by, from her bakery down the street, for us girls at work and to take home so we can enjoy them over the weekend.

"Lisa said I should come check on you. Something about last night?"

"I'm going to kill her," I mumble.

"Well, from the glow and the plastered smile I think I can guess." She squeals which makes me squeal unintentionally.

"Oh Saylor, it was amazing, and he was so great and gentle and caring."

"I know you're filling in for Cammie, so when do you take lunch? You can share all the elusive details." She checks her watch, and I see that my client should be here any moment.

"I'm at one today, what about you?"

"I'll tell the staff that I'm needed then too. I'll swing by and we'll hit up the café around the corner."

"Sounds good."

"Knock, knock!" We hear from the door, and it's the owner

of the spa and Saylor's grandmother, Sharolyn. I've called her Glammy since I was nine and she took care of me while dad was away on deployment, but when we are at work I call her by her given name.

"Hey Glammy!" Saylor greets, hugging and kissing her grandmother. She opens the top of my goodie box and offers her croissant.

I come over, giving her the same treatment. She's always dressed to impress. She's got on a black lacy top with a long leopard skirt that has a wide thick belt around her middle. She has short spiky hair that you see in magazines, and she is the essence of beauty. Glammy never leaves the house without accessorizing every inch of her body. People are always stopping her on the street or in a store, complimenting her style. I can only hope to achieve such a look.

"What are you girls up to today?" Glammy asks.

"I stopped by to check on Everly and see if she can have lunch later," Saylor tells her.

"That's great. Listen, I wanted to run something by you really quick, and I want you to really consider it," she looks over at me.

"Okay? I've got about ten minutes before my first client if you want to tell me the short version," I say, knowing that Glammy can be long-winded when it comes to her stories.

"Grandpa Alan and I were talking the other night. We've had an offer for someone to buy out all our spas, and I think we might take it. We really want to be in Montana more and this will enable that to happen."

"Oh, really," I say, a little disappointed that things will change around here soon.

"Well, we said that we might take it if they don't include this location," she pauses for a moment. "We want you to have this place and run it, dear. We've been so proud of how much you've grown over the years. You've got a really good head on your shoulders, and I think you could really flourish."

"Uhh…" I'm speechless.

"Everly this is fantastic!" Saylor cheers.

"Are you sure, Glammy?" I ask, losing all professionalism. "You'd make millions off this as part of the sale."

"What good is it if I can't give it to my girls and watch as they live out their dreams. We may not share DNA baby girl, but we have always thought of you as our other granddaughter."

Tears fill my eyes as she says this. "I love you so much, thank you!"

Saylor pulls all three of us into a hug as I let my emotions out. I couldn't be more grateful to have them and Saylor in my life.

"I'll have Reese start showing you the business side of things next week," Glammy says when we pull away. "I've got to go but I'll see you on Monday for our lunch date and we can discuss the details a little more. You girls stay out of trouble." She walks out with a wave and goes down the hall.

"Ohmygosh! I'm so happy they are doing this for you," Saylor says excitedly.

"I can't believe Glammy just told us that," I say still in shock.

"Believe it," she says as she looks down when her phone buzzes. "I've got to get to the bakery." She comes over and gives me a hug before she makes for the door, but turns when she's crossed the threshold.

"This is a good look for you Everly. Whatever this guy is doing, I hope it sticks." She giggles and I'm not sure why. "And I don't just mean in you."

"Saylor!" I chide her when it sinks in, and I get the double meaning behind her words. "You're going to divulge about your new guy too." I point my finger at her, giving her a knowing look.

"Later, slut!" She calls out with a wink, then she's gone with the door closed behind her, and I'm back to my serene room with soft lighting and music.

The light above the waiting room comes on and finally pulls me from my thoughts of last night and what Glammy just informed me. I really need to focus on work and stop thinking about all the ways Linc devoured my body. I wonder if I'll always feel like this, or if it's because it's my first time. Shaking my head to get myself back on track, I tap on the waiting room door to let the client know I'm ready for them.

I make my way over to the counter to wash my hands and gather up the lotion that helps with tension, when I hear the door close. Turning to introduce myself, I see that no introductions are needed.

"Oh, I didn't realize that you'd be my new client," I say a little taken back because I'm shocked at her standing here in my room. We haven't seen each other since that day over a month ago.

"I'm everywhere, or don't you see my face on billboards across this town or in the news," Linley Lewis bites, and I can tell this isn't going to be a pleasant treatment.

Linley is standing inside the room, wearing a purple jogging suit with a baggy jacket. It seems a little hot considering LA weather is already in the low eighties this morning.

"Miss Lewis, I'm here at my job working. If there is something personal that you'd like to discuss I'm sure we can meet after hours, but this isn't the time nor place to have a scene." I'm trying to be as professional as possible.

"Oh, we're going to talk. Well, I'm going to be the one doing all the talking at least."

Her words confuse me, but in an industry like ours where the client is always right, I don't really have a choice, and I hope that the next fifty-five minutes goes by quickly. The last thing I want is for the spa to gain any negative attention. Even being friends with the owner's granddaughter and them helping watch after me while my dad was on a mission, I'd never take advantage of our relationship to leverage to secure my job, if I'm in the wrong.

Linley moves to stand in front of me, leaving the massage table between us. Her eyes are wild, and I swear they look glazed over.

"If you'll remove your jacket we can get started." I gesture to her heavy coat, but she doesn't make a move to remove it. "Is there a certain area that needs more attention?"

Instead, Linley brings her right hand to her pocket and pulls something out.

Oh my God!

"I don't think I'm in the mood for a massage today," Linley sneers, tightening her grip on a metal pipe, the length of my forearm. "I wanted to give you a message."

My body starts to shake as my mind tries to wrap around what it is seeing. All the joy and bliss I was feeling a few minutes ago has left my head, while dread and panic settles in its place.

"Wh-what are you doing Linley?" My hands go up in front of my body in a surrender gesture.

"I've come to take back what was mine. What was stolen from me."

Linley makes a move to the top of the table, and I mimic her steps and head to the bottom of the table. Looking over her shoulder I realize my mistake. I've now put a greater distance between me and the exit; the only way out is having to go right by Linley.

"I've not taken anything from you Linley, I swear," my voice is void of confidence and quivers as I try to figure out how to get out of this situation.

"Liar! You've taken the one thing from me that was the most important."

"Linley, you have an amazing career. You're on every magazine cover and have all kinds of deals working for you."

"You think that will last forever? The rules of the game are to strike while the iron is hot because there is always a newer, younger, thinner girl waiting in the wings to take everything from you. I have an expiration date. We all do. Lincoln was my meal ticket when modeling fizzles out. He was waiting for me to come back from Milan for us to be together, but you ruined it. All of it!" She bangs the pipe on the table. Her voice is starting to get louder, and I can sense her desperation. Whatever she's possibly taking is putting her on edge, or she's having a full-blown mental breakdown.

"Please Linley, put the pipe down and we can walk out of here as if nothing happened. I won't say a word and we can both pretend this never happened." I plead. "Linc can come and speak to you, and y'all can work it out."

She has a manic laugh, and it sends shivers up my spine.

"How much is he paying for your time? Surely, it can't be as much as he pays me for mine," she starts rambling and what she's saying is confusing. Linc isn't paying me but why did she say he pays her? "Blaire hooked me up with Lincoln after I did my first campaign for the covers of several magazines and landed the biggest perfume ad. She apparently only allows the bigger models to be on the arm of Lincoln since he pays top dollar for us. The sex after is quite a bonus, isn't it. He sure knows how to use his dick."

What is she talking about? Why would Lincoln pay for sex

or pay to have models be on his arm? Bile threatens to come up at her words and the room feels like it's closing in.

"Blaire puts us through the wringer when it comes to him. She only wants the best for him, but I think it's because she's fucking him on the side too," Linley continues to spew more and I know I need to get the hell out of here. She is a ticking time bomb, ready to explode, and I don't want to be anywhere near her when she does. "There's rumors we know of, but no one knows for sure. I just know from my own experience what a great lay he is. Has he spanked you up yet or called you his good girl? Drea said the same when she was his arm piece before me." She gives this salacious look like she's finally gotten under my skin, and I hate to think of him with others. Especially since we just shared our first time together last night.

I'm sweating all over my body and my heart rate is so high that the vein in my neck is throbbing. I've got to get out of this room or it's not going to end well for me. I'm running out of options and talking with her is like pleading with a concrete wall. She's beyond listening to reason and it's now or never to make a move.

Pushing off from the table and giving it a hard shove, I'm able to make her stumble back as I make a break for the door.

"HELP! SOMEBODY HELP ME!" I'm screaming at the top of my lungs as the exit door to the main hallway is getting closer and closer. Help is just on the other side as long as I can make it there. "HELP!"

The words escape me but all too soon, as my feet are tangled in my rolling chair that was placed under the massage table. Linley must've pushed it over to stop me from making it to the door. I stumble and my hands catch the ground before my face does. I groan as my wrist buckles from the sudden weight of the fall.

"Did you think I'd let you leave so easily?" Linley spits as she shoves my shoulder so that I'm now flat on my back. Her feet straddle my hips as she stands above me with the pipe still glued in her right hand. "The only way for us to be together is for you to be out of the picture."

"Please, please don't do this. He's yours, you can have him," I beg. I'll say anything at this point.

"Too late."

"This will ruin you if you don't let me go, Linley," I plead. "You'll go to jail for this."

"Everyone loves me. No one will ever believe that I did something like this. I'm the most sought-after person in the world," she delusionally says. "Which means I can get away with murder."

Linley raises her arms, and I let out the loudest earth-shattering scream as the pipe comes raining down. My arms shoot up to try and block the impact that's coming for my head, and I feel a crack to my forearm as a white searing pain shoots through me. Linley repeats the action again and, even though my arm is on fire with pain, the next blow seems to hurt even more as she hammers my hand and fingers as I continue to block her hits.

Off in the distance, I hear screaming but I can't think or take my eyes off of Linley, who's continuing to pummel me. My body must be in shock because the blood that's splattered on her makes me think I'm watching a bloody murder scene at the movies. All too soon, my arms can't hold up any longer and I think my life is about to end with the next hit. My eyes are blurry, and slowly closing. I feel my body try to curl in the fetal position on instinct, but I'm not sure at this point.

This is it, I'm dying on the floor at my place of work over a man who'd taken my virginity last night. A jealous ex is going to kill me because I fell in love with the wrong man.

For a brief second, my eyes focus on Linley for the last time.

She looks like a crazed lunatic with splatters of my blood sprinkled across her pale face. *Is that all from me?* Her eyes are completely dilated and she's sweating like a stuck pig, huffing and out of breath. She must notice that my arms can't support and block her attack because she gives a satisfying smirk before she raises the pipe one final time. My eyes start to close as I follow the movement of the pipe on its way down. It all happens so fast that my eyes can't stay open any longer. They close before the pipe lands on my head, and I'm pulled into a black oblivion where my pain stops.

CHAPTER TWELVE

'm sitting in my office, leaning back in my leather chair, staring out my glass window into the city. Thoughts of last night filter in and consume every inch of my attention; I stopped trying to work right after I sat down hours ago. Hanging around the apartment had me pacing while waiting until Everly was done with work, so I thought I'd head into the office to try to calm my nerves for a few hours.

The first thing I did was make a call to a florist and have twenty-four red roses sent to Everly's work this morning. I wanted to make sure she knew I was thinking of her today. The florist was shocked at the number of roses but didn't mind since the price tag was enormous, with such short notice. I made sure the note was to my satisfaction before getting off the phone.

Last night was by far the best of my life. Two dozen red roses for every hour of today that you are in my thoughts. I'll pick you up after work.

Love,

Linc

Last night was amazing. No, more than amazing; it was magnificent, heart-stirring, spine-tingling. Everly was extraordinary, as she gave me the most precious gift a woman could give a man. Having lost my own virginity junior year in high school, I couldn't appreciate the value of it at the time and I truly wish it was something that I could've given to her as well. But I'll give her something that is just as precious. My love and heart. Something that no one has ever been given. I knew the moment I saw her at the courthouse, and then again at the bar that first night, that this woman would change me forever. She has become my whole world in such a short amount of time.

"Mr. Thorne, Anne is here to have a word." Alex, the weekend secretary, interrupts my thoughts of Everly. I guess I need to get back on track so that I can get out of here on time to meet up with my angel after work.

"Send her in."

Anne, one of the newest interns at the firm, has done well for herself. She's a Stanford graduate and had impeccable references from her professors and some of my colleagues. She's got a bright future ahead of her as long as she stays focused and continues to work hard. I have no doubt that we'll be offering her a position at the end of her internship.

"What can I help you with today?" I ask and shuffle some papers on my desk to organize my newest case.

"Well sir, Chandler is on vacation and Rich is out sick today, so I wasn't sure how the chain of command went after that," she says as she thumbs open her notebook. "I received a message from the police station saying one of our clients has been brought in and wanted to make sure that the right attorney was informed."

"Sure," I lean back in my chair and think if we have a procedure in place if both attorneys are out. Normally one is always there to answer the calls on the weekends. I'll have to speak with HR about that one. Quickly, I make a note on my pad next to my phone. "I'll have to check myself, Anne. Who is the client, and I'll see what I can do and who'll handle it for you?"

"Of course, Mr. Thorne. The client is," she looks down and pulls the notebook closer. "Linley Lewis. She first showed as your client but was then assigned to Chandler and then to Rich in the event he was not available."

"Linley Lewis?"

"Yes, sir."

"What are the charges against her?" I'm confused but I know we don't have any other client with that name; it must be her.

Anne turns the page then brings her glasses down from the top of her head. Maybe Linley was busted for drugs or driving while intoxicated. It wouldn't be the first time that this has happened in our city or in our client roster.

"The officer I spoke to listed assault with a deadly weapon, attempted homicide, aggravated assault, resisting arrest and injury to an officer."

What in the hell?

"Linley Lewis. Our client that's a model for Blaire Hutchins' modeling agency?" I ask again, to make sure I'm hearing and understanding her correctly. "The one whose face is on the billboard down the street. That Linley Lewis?"

"Yes, sir. The officer was adamant that she is our client."

"Give me the information and I'll see what I can do." I wave her over to get her pages in the notebook and then send her on her way.

Two seconds later, I'm phoning Olivia.

"Hey, I need a favor."

"Don't you always." She huffs. "What now? I thought you were out of the office until Monday?"

I tell her what Anne just gave me and have her handle it. Olivia knows quite a few officers down at the precincts so she's more likely to get better details than me.

Thirty minutes later, I'm elbow deep in researching a potential new corporate client when Olivia rushes in, banging the door against the wall.

"Thanks for knocking," I sarcastically say but her face shuts me up. I've never seen Olivia white as a ghost and she's trembling.

"Lincoln," she gasps. Her lips are opening and closing but nothing is coming out.

"What is it Olivia? What's wrong?" Jumping up from my seat, I rush over to where she's standing by the front of my desk.

"I-I just got off the phone with a friend down at the station."

"Okay?" I cautiously say. It takes a lot to trip Olivia up so this must be colossal. "What did you find out?"

"Linley is in a lot of trouble, but that's not what I'm concerned about." She pauses and the anticipation is killing me.

"Okay, so spit it out."

"It's the person Linley assaulted."

The silent pause has me even more confused. Why is Olivia all worked up like this? We handle cases like this every day.

"Let me guess, a cameraman or producer or some other model who took her position at the agency." I raise my eyebrows for her to continue, as I'm not one to play guessing games at work. My time could be spent doing other meaningful tasks.

"It was Everly, Lincoln. Everly Bryant was listed as the victim."

There are moments in life where you feel the world stop. Your body takes a pause to try to digest the information you've just been given. For some, that moment lasts mere seconds, but for others it can be up to hours before it registers back to normal.

"What? Who-who told you this?" I'm sure I heard her wrong because it couldn't be Everly. My Everly. My angel that I just sent a text to this morning. The woman who woke up in my bed after the glorious night we'd spent together.

"I spoke with a contact who works closely with the chief. She gave me the details from the preliminary report that was filed at the scene."

"The scene?" I think I've lost all faculties of reasoning. I can't even compute what she's saying. Like I'm having an out-of-body experience.

"According to the initial statements, Linley made an appointment to have a massage by Everly under a pseudo name. Several minutes after ten, screaming and crying for help was heard coming from a massage room. A worker rushed in and found Linley standing over Everly with a metal pipe, beating her while she was on the ground. Security, by the name of Bubba, came in and tackled Linley to the ground right when she came down and hit Everly in the head. He was able to get to her fast, so the hit to the head wasn't as hard as it could've been if he hadn't stepped in, according to the officer. Bubba then pinned Linley down, holding her there until the police arrived."

I can't move.

I can't breathe.

All the oxygen from the room feels like it's been sucked out and I can't breathe. I start to tug at my tie and collar to gain some relief, but I find none.

"Wh…how is—"

"The officers responding to the call said it looked like a fucking bloody massacre. They arrested Linley as the paramedics were rushing Everly to the hospital." Olivia clamps her hands firmly on my shoulders and gives me a shake.

"Is this a joke? Are you messing with me?" I finally focus and my eyes land on Olivia. "How did this happen?"

"I think we need to get to the hospital, Lincoln. I'll drive you."

I nod because for the first time in my life, forming words isn't happening at the moment.

"Is she? They said attempted homicide, so does that mean—" I can't even finish the sentence because I don't want to get my hopes up.

"We won't know until we get to the hospital and find out, but we need to move fast."

She grabs my phone and jacket and somehow, we manage to walk to the elevator and get in her car and into a parking space at the hospital before I can even blink. It's like I've walked into a nightmare I can't wake from.

"Let me do all the talking" Olivia whispers as we approach the help desk.

An elderly woman, with snow white hair, sits behind the desk and looks as though she's about to fall asleep.

"Hello, we were wondering if you might help point us in the right direction?" Olivia asks as sweetly as possible, turning on her charm.

"Huh? Honey, you're going to have to speak up," The old woman practically yells, and it echoes off the walls.

Olivia pulls her lips into a tight smile then proceeds to try again.

"I'm looking for a patient." Olivia bends down and is almost in her face yelling. "Everly Bryant."

"Are you a family member?"

"This is her husband." Olivia points over to me. "I'm her

attorney," she enunciates each word so the elderly woman won't question us anymore.

The woman nods then starts to slowly type on the computer. A sloth would be faster at this point. I move to take the keyboard away and do it myself, but Olivia must've anticipated this and grabs my arm, stopping me.

"She's in surgery."

My heart actually stops and my knees buckle. My hands mounted on the top of the counter keeps me from falling in a heap on the floor.

"Fourth floor. Go through those doors and down all the way, hook a left and those elevators will take you to the waiting room. Flag a nurse down and she'll be able to help answer your questions." The old woman hands over two badges that say 'family', and tells us to place them where the staff can see them.

"Thank you," Olivia says, taking the badges and snagging my arm to get me moving. "You'd think the hospital would be a little more secure than taking the word of people and handing over badges without fully checking the people out," she mumbles.

"This is all my fault," I say once we've reached the elevators and are ascending to the fourth floor. Olivia has fastened the badge to my white shirt and is typing on her phone. My hands are raking through my short hair as panic sets in.

"This isn't your fault, you didn't tell Linley to do this so you couldn't have known what was going to happen." She pauses for a second from texting and looks up at me. "Right?" Olivia gives me an eye that says I better tell her if she needs to be the one representing me.

"Of course I didn't tell her to do this. I haven't even seen her in weeks," I demand, feeling heated that she'd suggest that.

The doors open and we walk into a stark white area with nurses crowded around a desk writing or on the phone.

"Excuse me, we were told to ask about Everly Bryant up here." Olivia takes over again.

The nurse checks our badges before typing something on the computer.

"Ms. Bryant is still in surgery, but I'll notify them that family has arrived."

"Thank you."

"Follow me and I'll lead you to the family waiting room, so they'll know where to give updates."

We walk down another long hallway and into a room with plastic chairs that line the wall. A few sofas are placed in the center facing in different directions lined up with the televisions on the wall.

"I've got to make a few phone calls but—" Olivia says after I find a seat, but the door opens and a man comes in wearing scrubs and a colored hair cap.

"Mr. Bryant, I'm Julian, one of the nurses helping with your wife." He shakes my hand, and I don't correct him. "Sir, your wife suffered a great amount of trauma to her left upper and lower arm along with her wrist, hand and fingers. Dr. Brewer has had to go in and put a metal plate in on her forearm along with some screws to stabilize the bone—"

"What about her head?"

"She's stable and has been cleared by the neurologist for surgery but we'll know more about her head injury once she's in recovery and awake." *Oh God, that bitch hurt her so bad!* "Her arm is broken in several places along with some fractures, but Dr. Brewer is working to set those bones. She'll be in a bit of discomfort for a while but that is to be expected given the trauma she's been through."

"But she's going to make it?"

For the first time since I was eleven years old, I feel out of control and that the world is trying to take everything from me again. In the short amount of time that Everly has come into my life, I feel like I have something to lose again. My heart drops to my stomach at the realization, and I can't help but return to that small boy who cried for days as he was carted away and taken to a strange place that was unfamiliar.

"We have every indication that she'll pull through, yes." He nods and my heart finally starts to beat steady again. "We also have a plastic surgeon working on her to stitch up the areas that were damaged when she sustained blows to the face from the object that broke the skin. He is working to make sure that minimal scarring is present once the healing is done."

"Thank you," I manage to squeeze out; my voice sounds so far away.

"Also, Everly's father, Tommy, has been notified and should be here shortly. He is listed as the next of kin, and not a husband, in her charts. You'll need to get with Mrs. Bryant about changing that once she is awake so that you are contacted first," Julian informs me.

He leaves shortly after and tells us that he'll be in later with another update, if the doctor thinks it might take longer than what was predicted. Knowing it might be a while, Olivia and I take a seat on the sofa, and process everything that has happened in the last hour or so.

My phone buzzes and I see Alex calling from the office. Great, what else could happen to me today.

"Mr. Thorne, I've had four calls from the police station and seven calls from Ms. Blaire Hutchins, all calling in reference to Linley Lewis. I've told them all that you'd been called out of the office on an emergency, but I'm not sure how you'd like me to proceed. The news outlets are starting to inquire now that a story has hit the gossip line."

Shit, this is such a mess. Linley is a client we represent and have for over the last year, but how can I when she's the one who put my angel in the hospital?

"I have let the police station know that we no longer represent Linley Lewis and have given a few colleagues messages if they'd like to represent her," Olivia tells Alex after she stole my phone from my hands. "Thanks Alex and as far as Ms. Hutchins is concerned, send her to Levi and he'll take her messages."

Olivia hangs up, handing me my phone back and then starts typing away on her phone once again.

"We no longer represent Linley?" I asked.

"Yes, as of," Olivia turns her wrist over and checks her watch. "Fifty-two minutes ago." She must see the bewilderment on my face as she continues. "As soon as my source told me that Everly was the victim, I started the process of finding her other representation. I had Kimberly draw up a formal termination document, signed it, emailed it and had her send a copy to Linley's house through the post office and then a copy over to HR."

"Huh," When in the hell did she have time to do all this when I'm just now getting up to speed on everything that's happened?

"Lincoln, I did what you would've done for me if I was in this situation. I've seen the way you are since meeting Everly and there wasn't a moment of hesitation when I found out she'd been the one hurt. It did cross my mind to send your father her contact information but I wasn't sure if that would make it even messier."

"You're right, how would it have looked if my father was

representing a woman who put his future daughter-in-law in the hospital." Something warms my heart a little talking about making Everly a permanent fixture in my family, but I shake those thoughts wanting to focus on right this moment. "This is an all-around conflict of interest nightmare."

We sit there forever, waiting for someone to come in and give an update, as my phone blows up with news alerts from the media.

JEALOUS LOVER?

~LA Media~

IT SEEMS THAT SUPERMODEL LINLEY LEWIS HAS FOUND HERSELF IN A BIT OF A PICKLE. OUR SOURCES SAY THAT SHE WAS ARRESTED THIS MORNING AFTER TRYING TO KILL A FORMER LOVER'S NEW GIRLFRIEND…

MODELING BEHAVIOR?

~Cali Tribune~

Supermodel Linley Lewis has been arrested and is being held in the LA County Jail. Witnesses say they watched as she was being handcuffed and escorted out of a spa in the downtown area, with blood splattered all over her. Our sources say that it involves High-Profile Attorney Lincoln Thorne and his new girlfriend. The happy couple has been seen all over LA recently…

The articles keep coming, as interest in Linley Lewis continues to trend on the media outlets. It makes me sick and I want nothing more than to have our PR team set the record straight, but I want to wait and focus on Everly and making sure she's going to be okay.

Blaire has been blowing up my phone for the last hour, leaving long messages but I ignore them all. Right now, I can't deal with anything other than Everly. She is my main focus and that is all I want to think about.

The door opens and a large man fills the doorway. He doesn't have any hospital attire on and from the look on his face that is trained on me, he must be Everly's dad, Tommy Bryant.

From what Everly has told me about her dad, it fits him to a 'T'. He's about my height but broader than a barn. He definitely fits the military man style with his short, almost buzz cut hair and not a wrinkle on his clothes. For a man of his age, he still looks like he works out hard every day; there's not an inch of fat on him. Definitely not someone I'd want to go around with in the ring.

From what I remember Everly saying, Tommy Bryant does a lot of work for the government on a consultant level. She doesn't even know all the things he does but it involves being a ghost on some jobs. He'll go without contact for months at times.

"Imagine my surprise when I arrive at the hospital and find out from the nursing station that my daughter is out of surgery and being placed in recovery." A knot loosens in my stomach when I hear that Everly is out of surgery. *Thank God!*

I go to stand to introduce myself, and Olivia follows suit putting her phone away.

"Also imagine said nurse saying that my daughter's husband and attorney are waiting down the hall, if I'd like to alert them of her progress."

"Mr. Bryant, I'm Lincoln Thorne, Everly's boyfriend and this is Olivia Blackwater, my business partner and friend."

"I know who you are; I've read all the articles on the way here. But the question is what are you doing here telling everyone that you're married to my daughter?" He demands and it takes everything for me to stay polite and not pummel this man after the day I've had.

"I knew that they'd only give me updates on her if—" I start but I'm cut off.

"Mr. Bryant, I'm sure this is all a shock to you as it is for us. We just wanted to make sure she was doing okay and be here if they needed anything until you got here." Olivia puts on her charm but I don't think it's penetrating this man.

He looks behind him, as two security guards are standing outside the waiting room.

"I think it's best if you both leave."

"I'm not going anywhere except to the room they place her in after the recovery room." I force myself to keep my voice level, but am failing. Olivia tries to squeeze my bicep to rein me in but it's not working. No one is going to keep me from my angel, especially her father.

"For all I know you were in on this attempted homicide and until Everly is awake and can make the choice, you aren't going anywhere near my daughter." Mr. Bryant looks over his shoulder and calls to the security. "Make sure these two aren't allowed anywhere near my daughter's room or else I'll have your job and sue the shit out of this hospital."

He leaves, going in the opposite direction of the nurses' station and I imagine that he's headed to the recovery rooms, where Everly is being kept. This is a fucking mess. Now I can't even get updates on how she's doing.

"We need you both to come with us," the pudgy security guard says.

"Don't make a scene, Lincoln, we'll get this worked out," Olivia tells me, and then gives me a push towards the exit, as she pulls her phone out and starts texting someone.

They lead us down the hall to the nurses' station and from the evil looks we get, I'm sure Mr. Bryant chewed their asses out.

We go down on the elevators and back to ground level, where the elderly lady at the help desk gave us our passes.

"This is as close as you can be unless you get on the approved visitor list," the other security guard says as they strip us of our badges.

I throw myself in a chair and place my hands over my face, leaning on my thighs.

"I've got a friend who works on Everly's floor. She's coming in for her shift in an hour and will get you in to see her." Olivia reads the message from her phone.

I perk up immediately. I swear, Olivia has connections in every corner of this state.

"Thank you," I say then launch myself at her, giving her the biggest hug. Olivia isn't one of those touchy-feely people so when she embraces me back, I know that she's got my back when I need it.

Two hours and fifteen long minutes later Sam, Olivia's nurse friend, is weaving me down the halls on Everly's floor. She's asked another nurse to distract Mr. Bryant outside the room to give me some time with her.

"You've got twenty minutes tops. I'll knock twice if something comes up and see him coming back early," Sam informs me.

"Thank you for doing this."

"I owe Olivia everything, so this is nothing." She shrugs, then opens Everly's door and we walk in.

The room is sterile, white and the smell of disinfectant permeates in my nose. Sam goes over to the foot of the bed and checks her chart as I take in Everly laying in the middle of the hospital bed. She's so tiny compared to the bed; she almost looks like a child. Her head is bandaged and she's got a row of stitches across her cheek. Her left arm is in a sling, propped up on a pillow at her stomach. Bruises are already formed on her upper body and it makes me want to kill someone.

How could Linley do this to her, to my angel? Everly would never hurt a fly and for something like this to happen to her is a travesty. I'll make this right. I'll make sure Linley is punished for doing this to Everly, then we can put all this behind us and never think about that awful woman again.

"You've got some time, she's been sedated but could wake. Remember, when I knock be ready to leave," Sam tells me and then leaves me alone with Everly.

I go around to the side of the bed, where she's not beaten blue or hurt, and perch myself on the mattress. She's got the sheet and blanket pulled up to her waist, with her untouched hand laying at its side. Reaching for it, I place it against my cheek, wanting to make sure she's really here; I feel warmth against my face. She's alive.

"I love you, angel," I say knowing she can't hear me or maybe she can, either way I want it out there. I do love her, maybe even from the first time we met. She's changed me to want to be a better man and that's what she'll get from me, from here on out.

Everly's lips start to move and a jumble of soft-spoken words whisper out of her pink lips. It's something I noticed last night she does when she sleeps. After the best night of my life, I stayed awake and watched her sleep until the sun began to rise. I wanted last night to never end; for us to live in our little bubble for as long as we could. Never did I expect my past to come back only a few hours later and try to destroy my entire world.

"What are you doing in here!" A voice booms from across the room and a door hits the wall, making the pictures on the wall shake.

"Mr. Bryant, I—"

"I told you to stay away from her," he yells and takes a step towards me.

Surely, he wouldn't try to start a fight here at the hospital.

"What is going on here?" Sam makes her way in the room and she's a little out of breath, almost like she ran here. "Our patients are trying to recover and yelling and screaming isn't what they need right now."

She throws an apologetic look my way then goes over to check Everly's vitals.

"I gave orders that this man wasn't to be given access to my daughter under any circumstance." Mr. Bryant shoves his finger over to me.

"Well, I just got on shift and have heard nothing about who is, or isn't, on the visiting list. You'll have to take it up with the night manager." Sam stands up to him and doesn't back down.

"I want you out of here. NOW!" He demands, his voice slightly raised to a deathly tone.

"Linc?" A soft voice speaks and if there wasn't a pause in between Mr. Bryant's rampage we'd have almost missed it.

"Baby," I gush, as her perfectly beautiful hazel eyes open with a flutter. "Oh, angel, I've been so worried."

I turn away from Mr. Bryant and give all my attention to Everly. She's looking around, lost but as her eyes focus a little more, she starts to tremble.

"Linc, I had the worst dream. Linley, she tried—" her voice sounds loopy like she's drunk and her eyes are glazed over.

"I know baby, but you're safe now and she can't hurt you ever again," I reassure her.

She looks down at her hurt arm and her eyes widen. She starts to take in her surroundings and she must realize that it wasn't a dream at all but did happen in real life.

Everly clutches my hand with her healthy one and starts to sob.

"She-she…I thought she was going to kill me." She wails and I carefully pull her to me and hold her close. We rock for a few seconds before an annoying voice interrupts us.

"Sweetheart, how are you feeling? The doctor is on his way," Mr. Bryant pipes up and I wish I could ban *him* from the room.

"Dad? What? How'd you get here so fast?" Everly questions.

"Sweetheart, it's almost nine in the evening. You've had surgery and are just coming out of it." Her dad informs her.

"Surgery?" She gasps then looks down at the gap I've left between us, as I didn't want to crush or hurt her any worse.

She takes stock of her wounds and I can tell she's still high from the pain medication and the anesthesia.

The doctor comes in, and must feel the tension in the room.

"Ms. Bryant, I'm Dr. John Brewer. I was the surgeon who worked on your arm." He comes to the other side of the bed opposite of me.

"Maybe we should wait until everyone leaves before we discuss her condition," Mr. Bryant suggests, implying for me to leave and it makes me want to punch the man in the throat. He's looking right at me but it'd take a team of gladiators to get me to move from my spot.

"What? Noo dad, Linc can stay," Everly finally speaks up after seeing what her dad was proposing. We lock fingers and I can tell it doesn't make him very happy that he didn't get his way. I kiss each of her knuckles, so glad she's awake and talking.

The next ten minutes, Dr. Brewer goes over her case and all the repairs he had to make; the metal plate he had to put in, the recovery time and the physical therapy that she'll need after making sure everything is healing properly. To her credit, she takes it all in even though I can tell she's a mess and wants to break down.

Dr. Brewer starts to leave but turns at the door.

"Ms. Bryant, there are some officers out in the hall that would like to ask you some questions. I've told them that you needed your rest but if you're up for it I can send them in."

"Oh. Umm, I think that would be fine I guess." She's overly tired. I can tell by the way her eyes can barely stay focused and open.

"Let's wait until the morning, once you've had some sleep," I offer gently. "You'll have a clearer head, once you've had time to rest."

"Sweetheart, I think you should talk to them now so that way you don't have to deal with it later," Mr. Bryant chimes in, making me narrow my eyes at him trying to undermine my suggestion.

"She needs some rest," I snap, trying not to bark at him. I counsel people for a living and this is the worst time to question someone. She's loopy and in the morning, she'll have a better recollection of what happened to her.

A warm small hand is placed on mine and I turn to see my angel staring back at me.

"It's okay, Linc. I'd like to get this over with."

"Okay angel, let me call Olivia to come up here to make sure everything is handled correctly."

I'm already texting Olivia when Mr. Bryant grunts his disapproval. Less than five minutes later, Olivia comes in with a handful of balloons and flowers.

"Thought we might need to spruce this place up." Olivia smiles at Everly and I move slightly out of the way so she can give Everly a small embrace.

"Thank you, Olivia."

"You're welcome." Olivia steps back and pulls her messenger bag off her shoulder, and collects her black framed glasses and a notebook and pen. She is now in attorney mode. "Okay, Everly, the officers are going to be asking you a lot of questions, sometimes repeating the same thing but in a different way. Answer to the best of your knowledge and if you truly can't remember then just say that. I'll make sure that they are aware of the pain medication you're taking. This might not be the only trip they come to ask questions so don't be alarmed by that. If for some reason you want to stop the line of questioning just say my name and I'll end the conversation immediately. Okay?"

Olivia is one of the best attorneys in the state of California. Hell, maybe even better than me. She's focused and driven and gets results, and that's why I knew she'd be perfect for my firm when I branched out on my own.

The two officers come in and introduce themselves as Detectives Everett and Smith.

"Ms. Bryant, thank you for speaking with us," Det. Smith starts. She's a tall blonde-haired woman and is all business.

"Call me Everly." Her voice screeches and I hand her a cup of water to help soothe her throat.

Mr. Bryant is standing off in the corner of the room messing with his phone as Olivia and I take up either side of Everly.

"Can you tell us how you know the assailant, Linley Lewis?" Det. Smith jumps into the questioning.

"I don't really know her. We met one time before, very briefly maybe three minutes tops, if that. I don't even think we were properly introduced," she answers. "I know she's a model and has her face on every inch of this town."

"Who introduced the two of you then?"

"Linc." She nods over to me and I give her hand a light

squeeze. She's doing well but I can tell she needs to rest. Her eyes are staying closed longer with each blink she takes. This is a horrible time to interrogate anyone.

"And you are?" Det. Everett condescendingly asks. He knows exactly who I am, his entire force knows me from all the cases I've represented from their arrests. I know this drill like I know my ABC's. The female is to speak with the victim and play the sympathy card while the male is to play the tough role.

"Lincoln Thorne, her boyfriend."

Olivia leans in and hands Det. Everett my card and I see the wheels turning. My name is nationally recognized for getting convicted people off.

"Well, that makes things a little easier," Det. Everett mumbles. "And how do you know Ms. Linley Lewis, Mr. Thorne?"

I tell them that Linley is a client and that we went to several functions together, as dates.

"Was your relationship sexual, Mr. Thorne, with Ms. Lewis?" Det. Everett asks as they both take notes.

"I don't see how that's relevant, officers," Olivia butts in.

"It is relevant when the suspect tells us that she and her fiancé, Lincoln Thorne, both conspired to commit this act," The detective states.

"Bullshit!" I burst out and jump up from my position next to Everly. "I would never do something like this and that bitch and I aren't engaged. She's a nutcase, obviously. We had an arrangement for those functions and outside of that we didn't see each other." My outburst has me shaking with fury. How dare she try and mix me up in something like this.

Everly goes rigid next to me and tries to pull her hand out of mine. *Not happening.* Mr. Bryant is eating this up, just trying to find some ammunition to get rid of me, and I think he's got his way in.

"According to her, you and her planned all this yesterday evening." Det. Smith reads from her pad and a wave of relief rushes through me.

"I think it would be better if we didn't do this here in front of Everly," Olivia says watching my angel, and I can tell from the frequent beeping of the monitors that this is upsetting her. The last thing I want is for her to endure any more pain or a setback in her recovery. "We'd be more than happy to come down to the station to answer any questions—"

"Can you at least give them your whereabouts last night?" Mr. Bryant smugly asks. He thinks he's got the upper hand but little does he know what he's asking for.

Looking down at Everly I give her a wink before training my gaze back to him. She knows exactly where I was yesterday evening and I can't help the satisfied smirk.

"I've got nothing to hide." Leaning down I give Everly a soft kiss to the temple then nuzzle her neck. "Everly and I were together from the hours of five-forty in the afternoon yesterday to eight-fifty." I pause as the detectives are writing down the information. Everly's dad is about to speak up and say something but I cut him off. "This morning." I finish the statement purposely leaving that part for last, as to make a statement to her old man that were together. All. Night. Long. "You are more than welcome to check the cameras at my apartment. We were there all night and didn't leave till this morning for work."

"Everly can you verify Mr. Thorne's whereabouts last night?" Det. Smith turns her attention back to my angel for confirmation.

A light blush flushes her cheeks and neck, as I know Everly is thinking about last night and how wonderful it was.

"We were together." Everly can't hide the smile as she says it and our eyes are fixed to each other's. She looks so tired and I hate that she even has to answer these questions.

"Including," Det. Smith looks down at her pad and flips a few pages. "The hours of six-thirty and eight-thirty yesterday evening?"

"We had dinner last night at an Italian restaurant before going back to Linc's place. I'm sure there is a picture out there because the paparazzi were everywhere."

I give them the name of the restaurant and they write everything down. We go back and forth with more questions and answers for several more minutes. Once they're satisfied with the answers, they pass us all their cards.

"We'll be in touch," Det. Smith says and they leave as nurse Sam comes in.

"It's time for some rest for our patient and her pain medication."

"I'll come by tomorrow, Everly, and check in with you," Olivia says, then leans down to give her a hug, trying to avoid her injured arm.

"Only one person is allowed to stay the night in the rooms," Sam informs us as Olivia leaves, leaving Mr. Bryant and myself. She's just pushed Everly's meds through her IV and I can tell she's barely hanging on to consciousness.

"Dad," Everly starts and my stomach drops, thinking she picked him to stay with her instead of me. "You go and stay at my apartment. Get some rest and I'll see you in the morning."

My heart grows two sizes as Everly picks me to stay instead of her father. *Stick that in your pipe and smoke it!*

"Sweetheart, I think I should be here in case something happens in the middle of the night."

"She's safe with me. I'll call if there's a problem, Mr. Bryant," I sweetly say and can't hide my victorious tone. *I'm an asshole, what can I say.* I make a show in front of Everly, getting my phone out. "What's your number?" He grunts out the number as he narrows his eyes at me.

"I'll be fine dad. Go and get some sleep." She shifts, trying to get comfortable.

"Okay, well, it's time to let her rest." Sam motions to Everly dad, towards the door, to follow her out. With a huff, he comes over to the bed and kisses her forehead.

"I'll be back first thing in the morning." He raises up, taking one last look at his daughter and then shoots me murderous eyes that says *I'm gonna kick your ass.*

The room is dead silent except for the sounds of the monitor that Everly is attached to once Tommy leaves. Sam made sure Everly had her arm propped up with several pillows. As I start to walk over to the most uncomfortable chair in existence, Everly stops me.

"Lay with me," she mumbles as her eyes are starting to close.

"I don't want to hurt you, baby."

"You won't." Her eyes are closed but she scoots over, leaving enough room for me to get in with her.

Weighing my options, it only takes me half a second to make up my mind. I climb in under her blanket, after removing my shoes and belt. Immediately, she snuggles into me, but softly whispers for me to remove my shirt. One thing I love about this woman is how she clings to me while we sleep. It's as if I'm her lifeline, her next breath, and I plan to make sure nothing changes that. Carefully, I'm able to remove my shirt and we settle in.

My thoughts drift over the day and how easily I could've lost the most important person all because of my stupid past. I recall the choices I have made and how they are now affecting my present and future. Starting tomorrow, I vow to purge those actions but first I need to come clean to Everly about my dating arrangements through Blaire's modeling agency, and how Linley and the others before her were set up. I also need to meet with Dale and see about getting Everly some protection. I'm a huge public figure and handle some of the worst cases that are played out on every news outlet. The threats I get weekly because of who I represent could start bleeding over onto her and that's the last thing I'd ever want. She's my main priority and that needs to come first and foremost.

"I love you, angel," I whisper in her ear as she sighs contently. My lips kiss the top of her head.

"Love you," Everly mimics. I know she's asleep but her confession grips my heart in a tight squeeze.

She doesn't even know it but she's changed me in ways I never thought possible. I've grown as a man, just being in her presence. Things that others have that I never thought was in the cards for me are almost in reach. We have a lot to weather through before then but that can be for another day. Right now, we need to focus on getting her better and protecting her so something like this never happens again.

CHAPTER THIRTEEN

Linc

Everly is knocked out for over twelve hours, only waking when the meds wore off. She slept like an angel beside me as I slept barely an hour all night. The horror of yesterday's event keeps playing over and over in my head and I've got only myself to blame. I'm the link here that caused all this. Everly would never have been in the line of fire with Linley, had I not started this relationship.

"You're thinking too hard," her soft, sleepy voice says, bringing my eyes from looking out the window back to her.

"Morning." Leaning in, I carefully kiss her split lips. They feel chapped but I'll never tire of feeling them pressed against mine.

"What were you lost in thought about?" Her eyes are wide awake and seeking answers. Answers I'm not sure I can fully tell her about. Answers that could make her hate me.

"Yesterday." I shrug and turn so that she has my full attention. "There are things I need to tell you that may be hard to hear but I want us to not have any secrets."

I have a feeling when Linley learns her story isn't adding up, she'll spill about our arrangement and all the ones I had before her, NDA be damned. Everly doesn't need to be blindsided by that and needs to hear it from me, and not a crazy-ass bitch. The last thing I want is for Everly to lose her trust in me.

"That would be nice," she snorts as if it's crazy to think otherwise.

She moves to sit straighter in the bed to give me her full attention. She winces as she moves and I hate myself even more because the choices of my past are the cause of this.

"This sounds serious, Linc." Her eyebrows crease inward in thought. "Was there something you didn't tell the detectives when they were here yesterday?"

I nod and she worries her teeth into her bottom lip.

Here goes nothing.

Or everything.

"Blaire Hutchins was my first client when I opened my firm. She took a chance with me when I left from underneath Dad's law practice. I thought it was the best thing to ever happen since Dad told me that I'd be crawling back within six months. She was doing well with her company and making a name for herself on the west coast. She owns a modeling agency and has some of the biggest names in the business now, all over the world. Representing her business was huge for my firm, and I was able to bring in a lot of high profile, big money clients as she introduced me to people here in LA."

"So, all your dates that you've been photographed with are all models from her agency?"

"Yes." I sigh a long breath, steeling myself for the next confession. "Blaire had suggested it would be a good idea, once my name was splashed across the nation after I won some really big cases, to have an arm piece out with me to give more of a shine to the public. It was a win-win for us both because her girls got their pictures taken and I was linked to beautiful famous women. Being splashed on the cover of media sites pushes more advertisement, which in turn meant more clients."

"I'm not sure I follow."

"Blaire came up with an arrangement for me to make sure to try out a variety of her models that were having a hard time getting some of the big contracts. After I started to become a really big name in the news defending high profile cases, she'd send me some of the newer up and coming models and they'd get a photo with me out at a function after a huge win. Then they'd get signed by a top label shortly after."

"Okay, but being photographed shouldn't make a person flip her lid and want to kill someone." Something passes over Everly, like a light goes off. Her eyes widen and then narrow, telling me I'm not going to like her next words. "Wait, Linley said you paid for them."

Shit, this is a total fuck up. I stand from the bed and pull the chair over to the side of her bed so that we are facing each other. But it's also giving me a chance to gather my thoughts and how I want to answer her questions.

"Blaire and I had an arrangement, yes." I lead with that again, hoping it will soften the blow.

"You either did you or you didn't, Linc. I'm not here to play your evasive lawyer games," she scolds me. "Did you pay to have a woman for an evening out?"

"Money was exchanged as per the terms of the contracts."

Everly huffs knowing my attorney side is coming out on the defensive.

"What about sex? Was that part of the arrangement?" She snaps. "Did you have sex with them too?"

"I don't see what that has to do with anything."

"Look where I am, Linc, and tell me that I don't deserve every little detail."

I knew she'd blame me for this.

My heart constricts, thinking of her hating me.

"Well? Don't stop talking now," she snaps. Her feisty side is making an appearance. The tone and hostility sparks my argumentative side. I haven't been questioned like this since I was eighteen and wrecked dad's car after I stole it one afternoon. My anger that I usually swallow down and keep hidden is seeping out of the carefully constructed walls I've built over the years, and it's getting the best of me.

"Yes. Is that what you wanted to hear? We fucked," I bite out before I can stop myself. "I paid to have sex with some of her models." I've never felt shame like this in my life and I don't know how to deal with it. The reasonable part of me knows what she is starting to imply and that shame is pressing down on my chest hard, making my breathing come out heavy. I've always rationalized it by thinking that I'm not the first man to have an arrangement for publicity.

"What I want to hear from you is the whole truth and not the summed-up version that you pick and choose to tell me. I asked you that first time we ran into the psycho and you made it seem very different. You have to see that, right? You may think sex was just a transaction between two parties but, for some women, it has a deeper meaning. Obviously Linley thinks so too."

"It meant nothing. We went to a function, had our picture taken, networked with businessmen, fucked and money was transferred, then we went our separate ways."

My breathing is labored at the end of my rant. She wanted all the nitty gritty details so here they are all out in the open.

"What about Blaire?"

Her question throws me for a loop and at first, I don't understand.

"What about her?"

"Did the two of you have a contract? Or was it all for free, like a two for one special?" How does she know about Blaire and I? "Linley made sure to tell me all the nasty rumors swirling around. Did you pay to have sex with her like all the other prostitutes, or was she free?"

"They aren't prostitutes," I begin to defend but she cuts me off. What she's implying is making it sound dirty.

"You can skin a rabbit a dozen ways but in the end, it still yields the same result. You paid for their time, and it ended in sex. That's prostitution, Linc. I may be high on pain meds but I still know the difference. As someone who has more degrees than me, I'd expect you to know the difference. Or are you in such great denial that you refuse to see it?"

"You don't know shit!" I lose my cool for the first time ever with her. The things coming out of my mouth are not coming across how I want, and I'm starting to spiral in a dangerous direction I might not ever be able to come back from. I've never been in a courtroom where I've lost my cool but here in front of the woman I love more than anything else, I'm starting to see that I'm losing her. I'm losing the biggest case of my life.

For the first time in my life, I'm on the receiving end of being interrogated. I've never answered to anyone except for my parents and now everything I've ever done is being questioned. I hate it. This is why I became an attorney; to have heated arguments and really get to the bone of the matter. Never did I think I'd be on the other end, especially by someone I love and care about.

"Of course not, because you've kept it all to yourself and even now, you're still keeping things from me," she yells. "I didn't put myself in this hospital bed so I think I have the right to know what your past is so that I can measure if this is all worth it." She waves her uninjured arm around the room to prove her point. She winces and it makes me feel even more like shit because she's right. My actions and past are the reason she's laid up here.

Just tell her.

I'm quiet for two seconds, thinking out my next words when she speaks before I can get my words out. Her face turns angry and it's the first time I've ever witnessed this side of her.

"Get out. You can keep your little secrets, I'm obviously not worth enough to tell the whole truth to, so leave."

"Wait Everly, I'll tell you but not like this. Let's get you home and better, and then we'll have this talk," I plead.

"That's just another stall tactic, Linc. I guess I'm just more invested in this than you are." She pulls the covers up towards her chest, shutting me out. Building a wall to separate us. Her expressions are closed off and I can't read what her thoughts are anymore.

My hands rake through my hair, desperately wanting to pin her down until she listens. "Yes, we slept together and no I didn't pay for it," I blurt out what she wanted to know, frantic for her to not kick me out like this. Not when we have so much to discuss to clear the air.

"When was the last time you had sex with her?"

"Does that really matter?" I take a step closer to her, I'm jittery and need to pace but the need to touch her is fiercer. The lack of sleep is fogging my brain and making me slow to process all of her questions. I want to tell her everything but not while she's here in an unfamiliar place. She needs to heal from these injuries, then we can tackle my fuck up.

This is reminding me of the time mom grilled Reid and I over who drank all the expensive liquor, after a weekend away for her and dad. We were so drunk, laying on the floor and couldn't even get up without the help from someone. She reamed our asses. The one thing that stuck out in that lecture was when she asked what type of example I was setting for Levi. What if something had happened; who was going to be responsible for him. That sobered me up. I didn't want Levi to grow up with the same shame and guilt as I did over our biological parents dying and not being able to help them. I always wanted better for him. Now that shame and guilt is bearing down on me all over again threatening to ruin everything I've worked so hard for. My carefully crafted life has now started to have an effect on my relationship with Everly and I'm not sure how to juggle all this.

Everly doesn't say anything, so I guess it does matter.

"Two days before we met. She came to the office for us to look over her building lease and when it was over, I bent her over the conference table and screwed her." I'm raking my fingers through my hair doing my best to be honest but when I look up, I know that I went too far. Shit, I'm fucking this up. "I'm sorry," My voice trails off but she just stares at me. It's as if she's seeing me in a new light. The scene that is in front of me will haunt me for the rest of my life.

"That's just great," her voice is cold and low. It feels like the temperature has just dropped twenty degrees in here. A shiver runs down my spine.

"Everly, I didn't—"

"I don't care who you were with before me, although it doesn't feel good to hear about your conquests. It makes me sick that I even have to question you about it but I know logically that you're eleven years older than me and have had a life." She starts to rub her forehead and I don't know if it's a sign of her nervousness showing or if she's getting a headache with all the shit I've brought on us. "What I care about is that you're in this whole prostitution arrangement—or were. Can't you see how this would look if it got out? My god, you're an attorney for goodness sake! Think of what this could do to your business. Linley already tried to tie you in on this assault with her. Don't you think she's going to sing like a canary when Olivia goes after her and throws the book at her?"

Wait, is she trying to look out for me?

"Everly, you don't need to worry about any of that, I'll take care of it, if it happens." My heart warms at her wanting to make sure that I'm okay.

"So, you see nothing wrong with any of this? This arrangement or anything? Can't you find women the normal way to have sex with? Or is it too much of a challenge or work for you?"

"It's not like that, you don't understand. This is how it works in our lifestyle, the more money you have the more available things become without all the hassle."

"Am I a hassle since we don't have an agreement?"

"What? No, that's not what I meant." I'm losing her, I can feel it. I wasn't properly prepared for this discussion and I'm saying things that aren't coming out right. "You're my everything. I love you Everly and want to make this right between us. Just give me a chance to explain. We just need to focus on getting you home and healed. This other stuff can be shelved for a later date to tackle."

The door opens and a nurse in green scrubs comes in.

"Good morning Ms. Everly. I'm Kasey and I'll be assisting you today." She has a warm smile but it does nothing for the freezing temperature in here. Everly is quiet and I hate every second that ticks by.

"I think you should go," Everly says as Kasey checks her vitals.

"I'm not leaving, Everly, we need to finish talking about this."

"And I need some space to think about all this," she snaps but her voice is starting to become shaky. Looking into her eyes I can see the moisture building in them.

Don't cry baby! Let me fix this.

Why does it sound so final, is she trying to say goodbye or something? Is this what it's like to have our first fight as a couple? My heart feels like it's caving in.

"There's nothing to think about—"

"She said leave," a firm voice from the door says and in walks her father. Right now, he is the bane of my existence.

"Baby, don't do this," I plead because I know if her dad gets his foot in the door, I'll never be allowed back in. "Let me go and get some real breakfast for us and then we can talk some more." I feel like my time is running out and that the buzzer is going to blow any minute now.

"I've got all she needs." He holds up a paper bag. "Got your favorite, Evie, from Saylor's little corner bakery."

God, I hate this man.

He places the bag on her food tray and rolls it between me and Everly, blocking me from getting close to her.

"Thank you for the offer but I think you should go home, shower and rest for a while, Linc."

"I don't want us to leave things like this."

"I just want to think for a bit, I'll call you when I'm ready."

Feeling like I have no other option, I concede. Never in any of my court cases have I ever conceded but for her with those pleading eyes, I'll do anything she wants. Even if that means walking away when I know I should stay.

I lean over the tray that separates us and plant a small kiss on her lips. There's no passion, just a soft peck that she leans in for.

"I love you so much, baby. I'll wait for your call." It hurts not hearing her say it back. "Just give me a chance to make this right."

She nods but doesn't say anything. With a last look, I grab my things and walk out of the room towards the elevator, but not before Tommy catches up with me.

"Stay the hell away from my daughter." He has my elbow in his grip, stopping my stride.

"That's not going to happen, *Sir*." I yank free from him, then proceed away from him so I don't punch the shit out of Everly's dad.

The elevator takes forever but as I walk onto it and turn to punch the ground level button, I watch Tommy stand there with a menacing expression that tells me he's going to be an obstacle I'm going to have to beat in order to get back to Everly.

Challenged accepted Mr. Bryant.

CHAPTER FOURTEEN

Everly

I watch the door open to my room and see my dad come back in.

"How are you feeling this morning?" He asks.

"About the same I guess," I respond and then look out the window.

"The doctor seems to think you'll make a full recovery after physical therapy." He plates my bagel and spreads out my favorite cream cheese.

"Thanks," I say as he hands it over to me. "Dr. Brewer said I can go home today after another head scan."

"That's good, honey," he comments after taking a bite out of his own breakfast. I'm not hungry for food, at the moment but I want to get out of here so I know keeping my strength up will help in the healing process. "Do you want to come back home with me for a while?"

"I don't know," I shake my head but stop when I feel an ache.

"A change of scenery might do you some good, at least for a week or so. You can veg out on the back porch and read. It seems like you have a lot to think about, from what I gathered between you and that boy's conversation."

"He's not a boy, dad," I respond. "That does sound nice. I haven't been to the house in a while."

Dad lives out in a cabin style house that backs up to a national forest. Saylor and I loved growing up out in nature, getting lost with the trees and the quiet.

The door bursts open and Saylor barrels in with a man hot on her tracks, who stops in the doorway. He looks familiar but with all the medication I'm on, I can't quite connect the dots.

"Oh Everly! Please don't ever scare me like that again," Saylor says as she rushes over to me, careful of all the wires.

"I'm fine," I say, trying to reassure her.

"They wouldn't let me see you yesterday at all. What the hell happened? I came to the spa at lunch and it was like a circus. The cops wouldn't let anyone in or out for hours. Bubba finally told all the staff what happened and I raced here as fast as I could. Glammy has been raising hell, not being allowed to be updated on your condition. I called and called and didn't hear anything after you were recovering from the surgery. Then they said visitors had to come back in the morning."

"Yeah, I'd say yesterday was eventful." I try and joke it off.

"What happened? Why the hell did Linley Lewis snap? I've always told you that bitches who don't eat more than carrots are crazy," she says again and then I remember the guy that came in standing at the door.

"Who's that?" I nod over to the door.

Saylor looks over her shoulder then hops off the bed, "Oh, hi Tommy!" Saylor says nervously for some reason. She goes over to him and they both give each other a side hug in greeting.

"How are you, sweetheart?"

"Good, I'm good." Dad looks over toward the door where the mysterious man is still standing and not moving any closer to coming in. "Have you spoken to my dad lately?"

Dad shakes his head, looking back, giving her his full attention. "It's been about six months since we last had any communication. He might be out on a job but he might also be underground, laying low. You know how he can disappear for long periods of time, needing to clear his head."

"That sounds about right," Saylor scoffs. "He seems to be unplugging longer each time." She leans in and in a low tone she says, "Do you think you can not mention the guy I'm with? The last thing I need is for Dad to cause a scene or do something before I've had the chance to sit him down and talk with him."

"My lips are sealed, honey," Dad says, rubbing her back in a comforting way. "Just know that if you need something I'm just a phone call away. You call and I'll answer, got it?"

Both her and I are used to not hearing from our dads for long periods of time, ever since we were younger. Being in the military can be hard when they go out on deployments or missions, but since my dad and hers retired years ago, we still go long periods of time without hearing from them. Saylor more than me. Dad usually is out hunting or fishing on the Honey Lake. Saylor's dad has gone off the rails over the years. His paranoia and demeanor has suffered significantly since the last mission him and dad went on. Both men came back different but Saylor's dad, Adam, withdrew from everyone.

As I'm about to ask the man, who looks vaguely familiar, to come in so I can introduce myself, Saylor pipes up after checking her buzzing phone. "I forgot I've got to run to the bakery. New girl just started a fire in one of my new ovens. I'll call in a little bit."

"I think I'm heading out to Dad's place once they hopefully

release me tomorrow," I tell her. "And I'm not sure where my phone is."

"Oh," she pauses for a second then leans down to give me a hug. "I'll tell you later about my man." She whispers in my ear.

"You better," I whisper back and give her a squeeze.

Once they leave, Dad picks up our breakfast and helps me to the bathroom. He must've gone and stayed at my place last night because he brought some clothes for me to change into.

"Saylor couldn't get out of here fast enough," Dad says as we wait for a nurse to come get me for my head scan. "Looks like both of you girls have met some boys since the last time we spoke." He raises an eyebrow letting me know that he wants to talk about Linc. He's standing at the foot of the bed with both hands holding onto the railing.

"I guess so," I say.

"Do you want to tell me about this guy that's professing his love for the entire hospital to hear in the heat of an argument?" He asks it as a question but I know that he's wanting all the details. "I want to know why he's the reason you're laying up in this hospital bed."

Since I've got some time before they wheel me back for my scan, I might as well tell him all about Linc.

"We first met at the courthouse when I was there to pay a ticket," I say and see dad's face turn stern.

"What did you do?"

Dad respects authority to a fault and has always tried to instill it in me to follow the rules. I do for the most part… except when it comes to my car. Speeding and parking tickets seem to be my jam ever since I got my license at sixteen.

"It was a small parking ticket and to be honest I didn't even see the sign that was marked as a no parking zone," I tell him.

He lets out a defeated breath like he does every time and I can't help but giggle.

"Every gray and white hair on my head is from you and stories like this," he jokingly says as he pulls the chair up the side of the bed closer to me, then takes a seat. "Then what happened?" He encourages me to continue with my story.

"Linc showed me where the correct office was and we talked for a bit. We met up later that night at a bar, where my friends were hanging out."

I tell him more about Linc and he asks me more questions about his family. When I finally get to the part that led up to yesterday, I'm thankful for an interruption.

"Knock, knock!" A woman's voice filters through the room as the door opens. She's wearing pink scrubs. "I've come to get you for a scan before they can release you back out into the wild," she jokes. She comes over to check my vitals before wheeling me out. "I'll have her back in a little while if you want to grab a coffee or something," she says to Dad.

"Coffee sounds good." He says, then bends down and places a gentle kiss to my forehead. "I'll be back by the time you're finished."

Later the next day I'm being carefully placed into the front seat of my dad's truck, ready to head out to his cabin. After a call to Saylor asking her to pack me a few bags of things I'll need, we hit the road. After many discussions with the doctor, Dad was able to get me approved to take such a long drive out to the cabin, with the promise to have a local doctor check me out within twenty-four hours. The nurses made sure to medicate me so that I'd sleep most of the seven-hour drive.

Movement jolts me awake as the truck comes to a stop in front of my dad's cabin.

"We're home sweetheart," Dad says, placing a gentle hand on my knee.

"Mmm," I grunt, trying to get my bearings about me.

Dad gets out of the truck and comes around, opening my door. He swiftly but carefully helps me out and up the few steps through the front door.

"Do you want to go to your room, couch or back porch?" He asks.

Even in my haziness from sleep and pain medication, the house is still the way it was when I moved three years ago down to LA.

"Back porch, please," I answer and he helps me to my favorite place in the world.

Dad shuffles us around the couch and table to the wooden door with a stained-glass window. Stepping down onto the deck, I relish in the calm and quiet as our backyard butts up to Lassen and Plumas National Forest. The sound of peace is such a contrast to the hustle and bustle of being in a major city.

This is where Saylor and I grew up mostly. Her grandparents had a place not too far from here, where we stayed when our dads went on missions. We used to run around through the forest, loving the freedom of the land. It wasn't until about six years ago that her grandparents' business expanded and they moved to the big city, opening several additional locations. By that time, Saylor and I were almost grown and wanted to explore what else the state had to offer.

"Let me go and get you some pillows to prop your arm up with and some blankets," Dad says, bringing me out of old memories.

I nod and lean back after he's made sure I'm secure on the lounge sectional.

"You've closed in the porch," I state when he comes back with a handful of items. I nod to the screen that separates the deck and backyard.

He carefully lifts my bad arm and places a soft pillow under it for support. "Yeah, the smaller animals have gotten a lot braver coming up to the back door. One morning I was pouring coffee and a raccoon opened the door; shocked us both," he chuckles and I do the same. "Also had a few run-ins with a mamma bear and her cubs. Thought it'd be safer to separate this portion and not worry who I'm going to run into having my morning coffee."

"Probably a good idea," I say as he places a thick blanket over my body and tucks it in for me.

"Take these pills and drink this," he hands me my medication and a bottle of water, then sits down beside me, throwing an arm around my shoulder. I turn my head and rest it on his chest like I used to do when I was younger. We sit like that for a while, listening to the animals and bugs in the distance.

I'm not sure how long we were out there but at some point I fell asleep and was moved to my old bedroom. Waking up, I look around and see that Dad hasn't changed a thing since I left for LA; everything is still the same from the paintings to my comforter. A light tap on my door shakes me out of old memories.

"Come in," I call out. The door opens as Dad peeks in.

"I was afraid you'd still be asleep. I checked earlier and you were sawing logs. Thought some lumber company had moved in next door," he jokes.

"Real funny, Dad," I say as I roll my eyes. "I can't believe I slept all night." I say, noticing the time on the clock.

"I just made some breakfast since it's time for your meds,"

he says. "It helps to have some food in your stomach when taking them."

"Okay."

"Do you need some help to the bathroom?"

"I think I got it. I'll yell if I need anything," I say as I slowly
stand from the bed and test out my balance. Once I've made sure
not to fall over or stumble, Dad leaves as I close my bathroom door.

When I flip the light switch on, I gasp at my first look at myself. The lady looking at me in the mirror is not someone I recog-
nize at all. My face is swollen and bruised with small cuts across
it. I've got a bandage wrapped around my head where Linley hit
me. I can't help the tears as they fall down my cheeks. What did
I ever do to her to deserve this? How could someone think that
harming others was okay? A sob breaks from my throat and I use
my good arm and hand to hold me up on the counter. My body
is starting to shake and I'm not sure I'll be able to hold myself up
much longer, when the door opens and Dad is there. He never
fails to show when I need him the most.

"Why did she do this to me?" I bawl, no longer holding in
my pain.

Dad gently holds my weight against his, and moves me out of
the bathroom and through the house, out to the back porch. He
settles me down and drapes my blanket over me from yesterday.

"You'll be okay, honey," he rocks me as if I'm nine years old
again, wondering why my mom left and never came back. "We'll
get through this together, we always do. You are so strong—"

"I- I don't fe-feel strong," I blubber into his flannel shirt.

"You will." He rubs my back until the sobs start to dissipate
and the tears stop falling. Dad leaves once I've settled back and am
comfortable, to get some breakfast and my meds. "Take these and
lay back for a bit. I brought out your reader that Saylor packed."

"Thanks," I say, then continue to stare out at the trees.

"Do you think you can tell your old man what happened fully, that led to you being attacked and requiring surgery?"

I cringe slightly, but know that it's of no use to keep everything from him. I've learned from an early age that when he is determined to find something out he will, one way or another. It also doesn't help that he has dozens of connections in the government to help him.

For the next twenty or so minutes, I tell him most of what really happened and why 'Looney Linley' attacked me. I told him about Blaire and what I think might come out in the media, if Linley decides to go to the press, so that he's not blindsided. He stays quiet and lets me get everything out.

"Well," Dad finally leans back in his chair, scrubbing his face with his hand. "What are you wanting to do about all of this?"

"I don't know," I answer, shrugging my good shoulder. I really don't.

"The good thing is that you have some time to heal here before you have to make any decisions. Clear your head out here and just relax." I nod, agreeing with him. "It sounds like you really like this guy," Dad says, with a raised eyebrow waiting for an answer from me.

"I do."

"I'm here for whatever you decide but I don't want you to rush into a decision or feel pressured until you've had enough time to process everything that has happened the last few days, sweetheart. If you want him gone, then I'll help make that happen and he'll leave you alone. But if he is someone you want to keep around and see where this goes, then I'll support that too."

"You sure have changed your mind and attitude since the

hospital. If I remember correctly, your overbearing side made its debut."

With a shrug he says, "That's what dads do when their baby girls are hurt and in a hospital bed. Protect first, ask questions later."

I hold out my hand for his and he takes it. "Thanks Dad. I know I can always count on you."

"You sure can, honey," he says, giving my hand a gentle squeeze. "I've got to run a few errands down the street, at the store, and to get you a phone replacement. Are you going to be alright here by yourself for two hours?"

I nod, "Yeah, the meds are kicking in. It's weird that I only just woke up not long ago and now I'm getting tired again."

"That's your body trying to heal itself. Listen to it and rest. You'll see the doctor tomorrow, to make sure the long drive didn't harm anything, and then we see Dr. Brewer in four weeks for a follow-up. I'll make sure you have all your favorite junk food."

"Thanks again, Dad," I say with a yawn, as my eyelids start to grow heavier.

"You never have to thank me, Everly. My whole life is about making sure you have everything you need." He stands, then leans down and kisses my forehead. "Get some rest and I'll be back with popcorn and chocolate."

The sound of nature lulls me to sleep before I hear the back door close.

CHAPTER FIFTEEN

Week One Recovery

"How's the arm today?" Saylor asks over the phone during one of our many daily phone calls.

"'Bout the same as it was three days ago. The meds make me sleepy but it does dull the pain. I'm starting to feel like I'm part of the living. I get to shower tomorrow so that's an achievement, as long as I don't get the sutures wet."

"I bet you smell ripe," she giggles.

"Dad's been a godsend. I think he's been around more now than he ever was when he was in the service."

"I bet," she agrees. Her Dad still vanishes for months on end without a word. I know it's hard on her sometimes, especially when my dad pops in occasionally to say hi when he comes into town.

"Have you heard anything from yours?"

"Nope, but I don't expect to. I sent him a few texts but who knows where he went off to," she scoffs. "Have you heard from Linc?"

"Verbally, no, but he is still sending little care packages every day," I tell her.

The first full day I was here, a delivery man came with a large box of goodies in it. It had a facial ice pack mask for my swelling, along with moisturizing products to hydrate the skin. There was also a pair of silk pajamas to wear that is easy to take on and off. The second day, the same guy delivered another box full of crossword and sudoku puzzles. He added in highlighters and my favorite pens, along with another set of silk pajamas to change into.

"Sounds like he's giving you the space you wanted," she says. "But still making sure you don't forget him."

"Yeah, I guess. I'm not taking as many pain meds now so I feel like I can focus on everything ahead of me."

"Just know that whatever you decide I'm with you."

"I know," I say. "How are you and your man from the hospital?"

She lets out a dreamy sigh, "He's great. I can't wait for you to meet him. I've got some big news to tell you but I want to do it in person and not over the phone."

"Is it good news or bad news?" You never know with Saylor. She can sometimes get herself in a pickle but think it's the best thing to ever happen to her.

"I'm not saying until I see your face, sweet cheeks."

"Okay, okay, call me tomorrow after work. I'm living vicariously through you at the moment while I'm laid up here."

"You got it. Oh, Glammy and Granddad are coming to see you next week. So, make a list of treats you want from the bakery and I'll make sure to send all the goodies with them."

"I'd love that. I spoke with Glammy yesterday about their trip up here. They were going to head out to their place in Montana in a few weeks, but thought they'd leave sooner to stop by and see me for a bit."

"Not having you down the hall is killing me, Everly," She states.

"We've never been apart for long periods of time and I hate not physically seeing each other."

"I know but I'll be back in three weeks. Think of it as a small vacay from being grilled about your secret new man."

"When you get back, and if you decide to stay with mister attorney, then I want to meet him."

"We should double date and introduce everyone at the same time."

"I love that idea," Saylor says as a timer sounds behind her. "Ugh, I gotta go. I'm down an employee today so I'm covering the slack."

"Kay, love you, bye."

"Love you too, bye."

By the end of the week, I had enough snacks and entertainment to last a month sent to me. A note came on the last day with my package. I was hesitant to open it but curiosity won me over. Not to mention that Dad kept asking what it said.

Everly,

I hope your recovery is going well. I've wanted to call so many times but I'm trying to give you the time and space that you asked for. Please know that you are all I think about and I want to make this right between us. I'll do whatever it takes.

I'll be waiting here at home for you when you are ready.

Love,

Linc

Week Two Recovery

A knock on the front door tells me that my daily delivery is here. Dad doesn't even get up to answer the door anymore unless the package is too big for me to carry. This week, Linc has had flowers sent with every box, with a note or random saying.

"If that guy sends one more vase of flowers we'll be able to open our own florist shop," Dad yells from the living room, as I open the thick wooden door.

The young man, Steven, who is definitely still in high school is standing there with another vase of flowers and a small gift box.

"Hi," I greet.

"I've got another delivery!"

I carefully take the vase and box, tucking it into my good arm and closing the door with my foot, as I walk back to the kitchen to set down the flowers.

"What did he get us today?" Dad asks with a chuckle.

Earlier this week, Linc sent a home healthcare person to come and help me take a shower since I had to wait until my incisions were healed. When Martha, the home health nurse, came, she was instructed to bring a set of fishing poles along with a full tackle box, so Dad could go fishing at Honey Lake while I got a clean body. Then Linc sent a lady from a hair salon to come wash my hair every other day and braid it, to keep it out of my face. He also sent over a therapist for me to talk to about what had happened the day Linley attacked me. I was reluctant at first but Dad thought it might help if I had someone to speak freely to. So, when she came back the next day we spent over two hours out on the back porch talking. She's come every day and if it's possible, I feel a little lighter every time she leaves.

Using the scissors, I open the box and find a new pair of hiking shoes in my size along with a note similar to last weeks.

Everly,

I've been researching a lot about your recovery and hope

Martha has been helpful this week. I consulted with several doctors on the steps to recovering from injuries like yours, to make sure it was okay to send her to help you.

This week has been a hard one for me. I never knew how much I needed you, not only you but your voice in my life. The urge to come set up a tent in your Dad's front lawn is strong and if I wasn't scared he'd shoot me on the spot, I'd do it just to get a glimpse of you.

I told you in the hospital that I loved you. I had an entire date planned that night on how I was going to profess my love and it came at a pleading time when it should've been more special. You deserve every special thing this world has to offer and if you let me, I'll give it to you. I love you Everly Bryant and the next time I see you in person, I'm going to tell you and show you. You might have some doubts but I'll carry us until you are ready.

With all my love,

xoxo

Linc

Week Three Recovery

The days are starting to move faster. Dad and I have started to slowly hike through our favorite trails. We go into town and eat at our favorite spots and I feel like this is the closest we've ever been in our lives.

The swelling in my face is gone with just some bruising still lingering. My arm is getting better and I'm not required to wear it in the sling as much. The cast is annoying and itchy but that is to be expected. I'm hoping that next week when I go back to LA for my check up that everything is healing properly, and that I don't have any setbacks.

"We better head back home in time to catch Steven. I'd hate for the poor kid to panic if someone doesn't answer the door," Dad jokes as we round the bend. We've hiked longer today than we did Monday.

On Monday, Steven dropped off an envelope. I thought maybe it was a gift card but when I opened it, it was a picture of us on one of our dates. It looked just like a baseball rookie trading card but with us on the front. On the back Linc had written the date and where we went that day. I'd never felt more emotional in all my life. Every day this week, I've received a rookie card of us during our relationship, and it makes my stomach flutter like it always does when Linc comes into the room.

Walking through the backyard, we take the steps up and open the screened in porch right when the doorbell rings.

"I'd say that was perfect timing," Dad announces, holding the door for me to walk through.

With a little pep in my step, I open the front door and come face to face with Steven.

"Delivery for Everly!"

"Hi, Steven," I greet.

He hands me the envelope, then heads down the drive to his car with a little wave. I don't even have the door closed before I'm tearing into the card. Inside is another rookie card of us but on the night we made love. We were standing right outside the restaurant. You could tell by the looks in our eyes at how much we meant to each other. On the back of the card Linc wrote the date and the name of the place we went. He also included in quotes, *"Best Night of My Life"* underneath it. Inside is the note I've been secretly waiting for all week.

Everly,

I love you, I love you, I love you.

You are the best thing to ever happen to me.

You light up every room you walk into. I've noticed this past week how much you've changed my life and how I now look at everything. Before it was all work and trying to see what next job accomplishment I could gain. When you came into the picture, it changed. You changed me. I look at our pictures together and I see a guy who is happy with his life and living to the fullest, and none of it revolves around my job. You don't care what I do for a living or how much money I have; you only want me.

I've made so many changes in the last two weeks. I think Olivia has had our office therapist stop by for a session every day this week. I want to be better not only for you but for me most of all.

I hope your recovery is going well and that you are healing, not only physically, but emotionally as well. I'm here if you ever want to talk.

With all my Love,

xoxo

Linc

CHAPTER SIXTEEN

Everly

"Everything seems to be healing just like we wanted," Dr. Brewer states as he looks over where my stitches were on my head. "You've got another three weeks in the cast, then we can look over your arm and assess whether or not we need to remove the hardware, or if keeping it in is the best option. I'd like for you to stay in the sling for one more week then you can discard it."

"That's good," I say with a smile. "I'm not in as much pain as I first was."

"Every week you'll start to feel it less and less. Are you still taking the pain meds that were prescribed?"

I shake my head, "I stopped fully about a week ago."

"Don't hesitate to take them if you need it but do take over-the-counter relief for the next week if it takes the edge off."

"Okay, sure," I agree, nodding, as Dad does as too.

I'm at my four-week checkup in LA with Dad. We drove in yesterday and stayed at my apartment. He helped me clean the place and we went grocery shopping.

"How are you feeling mentally and emotionally? Have you spoken to someone about what happened?"

I smile, "Yes, I had someone come to Dad's house over the last two weeks. I'm good; just a few nightmares."

"It's important to have someone to discuss that trauma with, whether a professional or someone close." I nod as he types on his keyboard. "Okay, well I think I'll see you back here in three weeks, and we can get you out of that cast and start your rehab to build those muscles back up. Karen, at the front, will set you up with an appointment. Continue to take it easy until then."

We leave the medical office and head down the street towards Dad's truck.

"Want to grab some lunch while we're out?" Dad asks as we pull out of the parking lot.

"Tacos are sounding really good right about now," I say as I point over at the food truck as we pass a bunch of them lined up.

The weather is perfect as we sit with our food at a table under a tree, not far from where Linc and I ate all those months ago.

"Alright, sweetheart, you've had your space and time and I've not wanted to push you the last few weeks, but what have you decided to do about you and this guy?"

I take a gulp of water and raise an eyebrow. "Don't act like I didn't catch those subtle remarks over the last four weeks."

He does his best to scoff with a mouth full of food. "I was just making observations."

"Oh really?" I start to laugh as I toss a scrunched-up napkin at him at his blatant lie.

"What's important is that *you* are happy and it's what *you* want. All the outside noise doesn't need to be a factor."

"Can it really be that simple?" I ask.

"Yes, it can. It can be whatever you want it to be."

"You know, I don't think you were this laid back when I was in high school."

His face grows serious as he looks over my shoulder, deep in thought. "Ever since you moved here and I've been at the cabin alone, I've had a lot of time to reflect on the last twenty years. I wasn't always the best father to you, Everly." I start to correct him but he holds a hand up to stop me. "I wasn't present enough in your life. Yes, my career made it difficult but I was so worried about making sure to provide what you needed and to put a roof over your head and doing what my country asked of me that I missed out on raising you like I should've. I was so thankful for Adam's parents taking care of you while I was away, but I missed out on the major life moments with you. On moments where you needed me to assure you that you are enough and loved."

"It's okay, Dad. I think I turned out just fine," I say as I reach over the wood table and grasp his hand with my good one.

"But it's not." He squeezes my hand back. "I want you to be happy and if that means you living here in the big city, then I'm happy. If you want to be with this Lincoln guy then I'll support you, as long as he treats you like the most precious possession on this earth. If he's not, then I'll be here to take up all your time until you meet the right guy for you."

A wave of emotion flutters through my body as I take in his words. It's hard to put into words, when all your life you've wanted your parent to be present and hear you when you need it the most.

"Thanks, Dad, it means a lot," I say, getting choked up.

The rest of the meal, we keep light as I point out all my favorite places Saylor and I like to eat at or hang out.

"Where to now, sweetheart?" Dad asks as we hop in his truck.

"Do you think you could drop me off around the corner? I think it's time to talk with Linc for a bit."

"Of course, honey. Do you want me to wait?"

"No, I'll call if I need anything."

"Okay, I'll be back at the apartment," he says as he pulls up to the front of the tall building. "Go put your lovesick man out of his misery," he cheers as I hop out of the seat and open the door to get out.

"Dad!"

"What?"

"Aren't you supposed to be giving the *'hurt my daughter and I'll break every bone in your body'* stance?"

"I did that already at the hospital," he casually says.

"Wait, what?" My voice screeches.

"This poor guy has spent the last four weeks sending you personalized love packages every day, living seven hours away. I saw the way your whole body lit up every time Steven knocked on our door. It brightened your day and I watched you checking your watch a dozen times an hour waiting for those deliveries, honey. You knew the second day up at the cabin what you wanted, but I'm glad you and I got to spend the last month together."

I can't help the smile on my face. We might not have had a lot of time together when I was growing up, but he still does know me.

"Thanks, Dad."

"Any time, Everly. I'm just a phone call away."

"Okay," I say and shut the truck door.

Dad waits until I'm in the building before pulling away from the curb. As I stand in the open foyer, I watch as dozens of people stream in and out of the lobby area in a hurry.

Over the last month, I've realized a lot of things between Linc and I. For one, Linc said that he loved me and that I was his everything. But how could such an intelligent person think it was okay to support modern day prostitution? And then not be honest about it. Saylor, of all people, was the one who told me that there might be something more going on that I didn't know about and needed to give him a chance to explain further. It was something that happened before me and that I shouldn't hold it against him. If we judged everyone on their past then no one would be given second chances. During our time apart, I learned one thing for sure; I love him. With my whole heart. I might not have a past but if I did, I hoped he wouldn't hold it against me.

"Can I help you, Miss?" A young man asks at the reception desk, at Linc's office. I hope he's there and we can talk this through. I miss him more than he can ever know and hope that we can work this out.

"I was wondering if Linc was available." He gives me a confused look and I remember that no one calls him that. "Lincoln Thorne, I mean."

"Do you have an appointment?" He's typing on the keyboard and looking at the monitor.

"No, but I'm sure he'll want to meet with me or at least know I'm here."

"Your name?"

I give him my name and wait as he makes a call.

"Someone will be down shortly to speak with you. Please have a seat." He motions over to the set of chairs.

Minutes go by and I'm starting to think this was a bad idea. Maybe he doesn't want to see me or has moved on. But that can't be right after all the daily packages and notes he sent. The elevators open with a ding and a woman dressed straight off of Rodeo Drive comes strutting off. Her skyscraper heels click against the floors louder than any other shoes. She screams money from the tip of her head to the bottom of her shoes. As she passes the receptionist her eyes hone in on me, bringing her to a halt. The lady does an about face, making her way over to me, not once losing eye contact.

"So, you must be what all the fuss is about," she states, her voice is dripping in hatefulness. It's like she views me as the dirtiest thing she could find on the bottom of her heels.

"I'm not sure what you mean or if you have the right person."

"Everly, right?" Her eyes narrow.

"That's my name, but I'm afraid I don't know yours."

"Blaire, Blaire Hutchins."

The name recognition sets in and it's my turn to narrow my eyes.

"Is there a reason for you coming over here, or are you just going to continue to stare at me trying to intimidate me?" I ask.

"I know girls like you, hell, I *was* a girl like you once. Someone who sees dollar signs and a pampered lifestyle. He won't be satisfied for long with a plain bitch like you. He's had the most exotic women on this planet. Surely you can see how you'd never measure up."

She's as smug as she is plastic from head to toe. What the hell is that supposed to mean, *girls like me?*

Another ding from the elevators, along with the pounding of heels, has me slanting my eyes over at the commotion.

Olivia rushes out as if her ass was on fire. She homes in on my location and makes a b-line for me.

"Gosh, Everly it's so good to see you." She swoops down and gives me a hug, being mindful of my arm that's still in a sling. "How are you doing?"

It's then that she notices the vile woman beside her.

"Ms. Hutchins," Olivia narrows her eyes ever so slightly. "I'd suggest if you're done with your meeting, you leave the premises and be warned to stay far away from my client." Olivia is using her *don't fuck with me* tone.

Blaire's nose flares as she whirls on her expensive heels, then makes her way over to the glass doors. Olivia watches as she takes her final steps out of the building, before turning her attention back to me.

"Oh Everly, I'm glad you're here. Does Lincoln know your back?"

I shake my head.

"No, I thought I'd surprise him but I can see he's occupied." I nod at the glass doors that the evil woman just left from.

Olivia looks confused then a shocked realization passes over her face.

"No, it's not what you think. Lincoln's not even here. He doesn't handle her or her business anymore."

"Oh, so he's not here." I feel a little bummed but then realize that he might have court right now.

"He's not here because today he sets aside time for his foun-dation," Olivia says in a hushed voice.

"Foundation?" I whisper back like we're trading secrets.

"Yeah, his *foundation*," she says it again, like I'm supposed to know what this means.

Finally, after giving her the *what are you talking about* look, she must know that I have no idea what she's talking about.

"Good God, hold on one second." Olivia fishes out her phone and tells someone that she's stepping out for a bit. "Come on, we need to get you over to him. Hopefully, it'll bring him out of his funk."

"He's been in a funk?"

"The worst. Ever since you went back home with your dad,

Lincoln has been moping around in the worst mood. A true grizzly bear."

Olivia takes my good elbow and guides me out of the building and into a waiting car with a driver. Once we're settled in and she gives the driver the address, silence fills the car.

"How's the arm healing?" Olivia finally asks.

"Good, everything is on track according to the doctor."

"That's good. On the legal side, everything is going as planned for the case against Linley. She's being kept under lock and key until trial. They are trying to have her evaluated but I'm not going to allow them to use the mentally unstable approach."

"Thank you for taking my case but you have to know that I can't pay for your services. I'd be more than happy to work out some payment plan up until now but going forward…"

Over the last few weeks Olivia has called and we discussed filing a civil suit against Linley. At the time I was all about seeking justice but the more I think about it the more I realize how expensive this could cost. Linley gets paid millions of dollars for her modeling contracts and could possibly make this case take years in the courts. I realize that this could get very costly and as someone who doesn't have a ton of money I don't think I can foot the bill for it.

"I'm doing this pro bono, Everly. I wouldn't take a single penny from you, even if you tried. This is something that I want to do and plan to see it all the way through. You've become a part of our little family and this is what we do for family." Olivia places a comforting hand on my knee.

"Thank you, Olivia. I seriously wouldn't even know where to start or how to begin all this court stuff if you hadn't taken over."

A short while later, we pull up to an older building that looks to be a warehouse of some sort.

"He really didn't tell you about this place?"

Shaking my head, I take in the brick exterior as Olivia tells the driver to hang out for a bit.

"It really is his place to tell you but the cat's out of the bag now, huh." She shrugs and pockets her phone in her suit jacket.

We start to walk up the few cement steps when she stops me.

"Has Lincoln told you about his childhood?" Olivia asks.

"He's told me a few things but we never went in depth on it."

"All I'll say is this, don't let the expensive luxury lifestyle fool you. He didn't grow up this way. After we grew the firm, he started this place but the bigger he got the more this place was neglected. Once you walk in there, you'll see what I'm talking about. Not many people know about this place on the business side, at least not the upper snooty ones. This is the one place he doesn't want recognition for. A place he feels like he really makes a difference."

Now my curiosity is at an all-time high. What's behind the brick and mortar that he keeps to himself? I start to make my way towards the doors when I hear Olivia call out to me.

"If you need me to come back and get you, call and I'll come." She opens the back-car door but turns back to me. "He really is a good man, once you crack his shell. Just give him a chance. He's been a wreck since all this happened, and I'm hoping you're here to reconcile and bring back my friend to the man he was after he met you."

With those parting words, she ducks into the town car and I watch as the driver pulls away.

Steeling a long deep breath, making sure to rid some of the anxiety coursing through my body, I pull on the metal knob of the door and walk in.

The front entryway looks as though you're walking into a gym. There's an older woman, maybe in her fifties, sitting behind a counter, typing away on the computer. As I make my way a little further in, a ding rings out and she looks up and spots me. A friendly smile forms on her face as she stands to greet me.

"Hello, welcome to SafePlace LA. I'm Erica. What can I help you with today?" Erica comes around the counter and extends her hand in greeting. Just by looking at her, I can tell she's a nurturer by nature. She has the voice and mannerisms for it.

Erica eyes my arm in the sling and tries her best not to show her appraisal of my entire body. My bruises have long since healed and Dad said that I finally have a glow of life back in me since we started our hikes in the woods.

"We have plenty of space available if you're in need of a place to stay for a while. The facility is amazing and we can make your stay here comfortable. Discretion is not a problem," she adds.

Oh whoa, back up. Oh goodness, she thinks I'm here to hide out or that I'm homeless. I'm guessing this place is a shelter of some sorts.

"I'm not here to stay Erica, but thank you for the offer," I kindly say. "I'm actually looking for Lincoln Thorne. Is he around here or has he already left for the day?"

"Oh dear, please forgive me. I thought… well, never mind, come on back with me and I'll see if he's done yet."

I follow her through a thick metal door, that she scans to get in, then walk down a long hallway with rooms filling both sides. I was able to see in one of the rooms and it had beds and dressers in them. After we take a right then left turn, we enter through another metal door that leads into a very large gymnasium. It looks brand new or very well maintained. The place is huge, offering a full basketball court, a place for kickball, batting cages, and a volleyball court on the far side. Off to the other side, there are more doors as we make our way over in that direction.

"Lincoln should be almost done," Erica says as we stop and she peers in after opening a door. "Come, you can sit in the back until he's finished."

She guides me in quietly. As we enter, I hear his voice before my eyes see him. My body lights on fire the closer we get to each other. Erica offers me a seat before she heads back out of the room.

"I know some of you want to give up but there is so much more out there waiting for you. I've been where you are and feel the same as you. I didn't have an awesome place to retreat to but I made it work. Made sure that when I woke up every morning that today was going to be a good day," Lincoln encourages the group of young kids.

He looks so relaxed, propped up on a wooden brown desk towards the front of the room. He's wearing a pair of black basketball shorts with a white sleeveless shirt that shows off his ripped arms. His hair is a mess and from the dark circles under his eyes that match my own, I can tell he isn't sleeping much. Linc looks in his element here talking with these young kids, as if each one is waiting with bated breath for his next words. He's so enthralled in speaking with them that he doesn't even notice that I've walked in.

My purse gets caught on my sling as I try to take it off and it tips over, making a loud noise as some of the contents spill out and onto the floor. I duck down to gather up the items, trying to dodge everyone's looks, hoping to be ignored but the scrape of several chairs against the floor sound out.

"Here, let me help you," a gentle voice offers, as a set of hands come down to help wrangle my pen and lip gloss that rolled away from me.

"Thank you," I whisper. The young boy who helped me hands me my things, then takes his seat again.

The room is eerily quiet and as I raise my head, hoping that

Linc is still in discussions with the group, my eyes fall on the man that's been keeping me up every night for the past twenty-eight nights. His shocked eyes stare at me, as if I'm a mythical creature. The full lips I haven't tasted in so long are slightly open, and his body is straight as a board.

"Everly?" Linc says in question, like he's not sure he believes his eyes. The group of kids have all turned in their seats with their heads snapping back and forth at us. Whispers start to fill the room but all I can focus on is the man who looks cemented to the ground in front of the desk.

"Hi." I stand from my chair in the back. Maybe this wasn't such a good idea and I should've waited back at his office with Olivia.

He still hasn't made a move from his spot at the front or said anything else, which isn't a good sign. I'm sure I could call Saylor to come and get me as soon as someone tells me exactly where here is.

"Guys this, Everly," he tells the room, not taking his eyes from me. I give the room a look and a small wave as I feel my cheeks heat from all the eyes on me. "Remember me telling you about her being in an accident a few weeks ago?"

"Yo, LT got a lady!" A voice from across the way sounds off and the room bursts in hollers and whistles.

"LT too ugly to have a lady that fine."

"Dude, I hope she's the new counselor."

"Sorry, but she must be here for me."

My face immediately burns even hotter, not only from their words but at this entire situation. I think I've read this all wrong and should leave now with my dignity somewhat still intact.

Turning on my heels, I secure my purse and start for the door to get the hell out of here and away from the suffocating room.

I'm almost to the door, when I hear Linc over the grumblings of the room I'm all but running from.

"Wait! Don't leave," Linc calls out and the sound of shoes jogging towards me has the hairs on my forearm standing tall.

I make it out the door and down the hall a few feet, when I feel his chest caress my back as his body towers over mine. I turn to face him and our bodies press together.

"What are you doing here, Everly?" Linc asks in my ear, where his lips almost touch my lobe.

I'm not sure if he's angry or what, as his tone doesn't give anything away.

"I... I had an appointment—"

He lets out a breath on my shoulder and neck, making the words in my head jumbled and not at all able to surface through my mouth.

"Twenty bucks says they kiss."

"You ain't even got two bucks to your name."

"Yo, shut up man."

The bantering must bring Linc out of this situation, as he takes a step back. I let out the breath I was holding and try to gather my thoughts. He walks back to the door and pops his head in.

"You guys go and have some fun today. Try and remember what we talked about. I'm here if any of you need me." He dismisses them as they mumble, leading out the other side door at the front of the room.

The door closes with a deafening click and all that can be heard is my heart pounding against my ribcage.

"Everly," Linc starts but I interrupt him.

"I'm sorry I came here. I should've called or emailed you, not just showed up…"

Two large hands press against my body, one on my uninjured shoulder and the other on my hip giving them a light squeeze. I shake my head to stop rambling; I've become a bumbling idiot.

"Baby, take a breath before you pass out."

I finally look up at his face and see worry written across it.

"Linc," I say but a lump gets caught in my throat and tears prick the backs of my eyes. I can't help the flow as they start to stream down my cheeks, but his thumb is right there to catch every one of them. Seeing him here in the flesh, after a month, is overwhelming me.

"Don't cry, baby. It kills me every time."

Linc pulls me in, careful of my arm, and holds me as I let the past few weeks wring out of me. I feel Linc lean down and, with a strong arm he picks me up from under my knees and cradles me to his chest while moving us. I bury my face in his neck and breathe in his scent. God, he smells like home.

"Tell me what you need, Everly." I hear the sound of a door open and then he has us seated with me in his lap as he slightly rocks us.

Looking up, I lift my head so that my eyes and his eyes are focused.

"You, Linc. I need you."

"Me?" He asks, shocked by my answer.

"Yes, you Linc. I need you." He starts searching over my face with his eyes, as if he thinks he's hearing the wrong words coming out of my mouth.

Reaching up, I cup his cheek and lean in close.

"I love you, Lincoln Thorne. I love you and I should've told you that before I left."

He swallows hard as his Adam's apple bobs.

"You love me?"

"I do. I love you with everything in me. This past month has been miserable, and I'm sorry for shutting you out. I thought I needed some time to think, but what I really needed was you."

"Oh Everly, I love you too. I thought I'd lost you after what happened. I'm so sorry for everything and not being up front…"

I place a finger over his lips.

"It's done and I know we have other things to discuss but right now I just want you to hold me for a bit, if that's okay?"

"Anything you want, baby."

Linc bends his head down and captures my mouth with his. The feel of his soft lips touching mine makes my body ignite and come alive.

A roar of noise booms through the hall, making us break up our kiss.

"I told you LT had game!"

"Where's my twenty bucks?"

"Man, I never get the fine ones."

Linc looks down at me, as the voices and comments carry from his group of kids who are creeping through the small windows of the door at us, and we burst out in laughter.

"Let's get out of here so we can talk," Linc says and stands from the chair as he gently places me down back on my feet.

"Are you sure it's okay to leave? Don't you have a class or something?"

"I'll explain everything at home."

Home.

The word has me feeling a lightness that I haven't had in a long time. Warmth filters over me and a flutter expands in my chest.

"Okay."

CHAPTER SEVENTEEN

Linc

Everly is laying down with her head on my bare chest fast asleep. We got home an hour ago and from the exhausted look she had, I knew she'd crash soon. I had her lie down for a bit and then we'd have an early dinner with just the two of us. She feels good in my arms and as I breathe her in, I eye every part of her. I had her change into some of my sleep pants and tank top to get comfortable. Her injured arm is carefully across my stomach, and I can't help the knot in my belly when I see the scars from the incident. How can a person do something like this to an innocent woman, who'd never hurt even a fly?

Linley is in some serious trouble. She was found with several illegal substances in her purse, not to mention the attack she poured down on Everly. She also assaulted an officer when she was arrested. Olivia is wanting the book thrown at her and I couldn't agree more. Linley has always thought the world revolved around her and that nothing could touch her. I hope a judge sees it our way and locks her the hell up. Olivia and I have a few markers we could call in on but are waiting to see which direction the trial is headed first.

These last twenty-eight days have been hell for me. Being forced out of her hospital room and told that she didn't want to see me again was like a knife through my heart. I'm not even sure how I managed to get home from there because everything was a blur. The thought of never seeing or hearing from Everly again was like being told she was dead. The finality in her words stabbed every inch of skin on my body. Olivia tried to reassure me that she just needed some space and that once she got a clear head that she'd call or come by, but as each day the sun rose and set, I was starting to have doubts. What if I'd fucked this up so bad that there was no coming back?

Finally allowing myself to relax, I tighten my hold on Everly and let my tired eyes shut. I'm just hoping that when I wake, this isn't some horrible joke being played on me and that she's really here in my arms.

"NO!"

A scream jolts me awake, putting me on high alert. My eyes roam around the now darkened room, as the sun is setting. Movement on my chest brings awareness to the sweaty mess in my arms.

Everly.

She's thrashing around but because of my hold on her, she's putting up more of a fight as the seconds continue. Scared she's going to hurt her arm, I gently untangle my arms from her and lay her on her back. I place my body down on hers to secure her in place and then lean in with my face to her neck, close to her ear.

"Baby it's just a dream, wake up," I coax, hoping to bring her out of this.

"Please stop!" She begs as her body shivers.

It kills me that she's probably reliving what happened with Linley attacking her, and it makes me want to hunt that bitch down and kill her with my bare hands.

Nuzzling her neck and telling her everything's alright seems to help some. I kiss her cheek and her eyes start to flutter.

"You're safe, baby. I won't let anything happen to you," I whisper and it seems to rouse her from sleep. Everly turns her head towards me but then looks around at her surroundings, as if not believing she's here with me.

"Linc?" Her voice is groggy from sleep.

"I'm here, it was just a nightmare." I can feel her heart racing and it pains me to no end. *Does she have them often?*

"It was… I thought…" Everly rubs her hand down her face.

"You're safe," I tell her again. "Nothing can hurt you ever again." I promise.

What I want is to wrap her in my arms and never let her go but I need her to make the first move. She's been through something that I'll never understand and can only sympathize with. The attack is something that she's going to have to overcome by herself and I can only be a body to lean on in the meantime.

"What time is it?" She peeks over to the nightstand at the digital clock. "Wow, I can't believe I just slept for five hours," she says in disbelief.

"I think we both needed the sleep."

Her hand comes up and cups my cheek. Looking at me, her eyes soften.

"You look tired Linc."

"I'm fine," I respond the same way I've done for the past month when anyone questions how I'm doing. It's a straight lie but she doesn't need to be worried about me at all when she's the one who was attacked and hurt.

"I can see you're not but I'll let it slide this one time," she says before removing her warm palm from my cheek.

"I don't want you to worry about me."

"How can you say that? You may not have been physically hurt but that doesn't mean that you didn't suffer in all this too."

How she can experience the horrific ordeal she went through and still want to make sure my wellbeing is okay, makes her the most amazing person on this planet.

"I love you," I say without thinking.

"I love you too, Linc."

My heart thumps rapidly against my ribcage and I don't think I'll ever tire of hearing that.

"How are you feeling? Have you been back to the doctor yet?" I ask.

"I saw Dr. Brewer earlier today and everything checked out perfectly. I go back in three weeks to get the cast off and start physical therapy."

"That's good," I say. "Are you hungry? I can order us some food and then we can talk for a bit?"

"Yeah, I think that sounds great," she says as her stomach starts to rumble at the mention of food.

We get up from the bed and I head out towards the kitchen to order from the take-out menus, as Everly pops into the bathroom. When she comes out, I've placed our order for pizza and settle us on the couch. I'm on one end facing her and she's opposite, mirroring me. I'd prefer for her to be snuggled up against me where I can feel her body but I know our talk is something we have to, in order to move forward.

"Ran into Blaire Hutchins this afternoon when I stopped by your office to see you," she says, staring right at me but not in an accusatory manner.

"Well that's not how I thought we'd start our conversation but we can if you want to," I cautiously say. "I haven't spoken to Blaire personally in almost two months. I passed her account off to Levi and another associate at the firm." I take a deep breath then lean forward toward her. "I want to say to you how incredibly sorry I am for the way I acted out when you were in the hospital. Everything was so out of control and I was so worried about you that I wasn't in my right mind. I was so panicked about what had happened and then relieved when they said you'd be okay. When you started asking me questions, I should've started from the beginning and told you everything, not deflect. I thought getting you home safe and starting your recovery was more important than what was being thrown at me."

"I get that you have a history before me, Linc. I really do. It comes with the territory of dating an old man," she says with a smirk and I can't help but clamp down on her ankle with one of my hands and use my other one to tickle the bottom of her foot.

"Easy on that old man business," I playfully chastise, making sure she doesn't hurt her injured arm in our playfulness as we laugh. "I'd be careful with my words when you're down a good limb to fight back."

"Okay, okay you win that one," she concedes with a giggle and it's music to my ears. It's nice to see her happy like she was before everything went to shit.

"You may continue then," I say, then release her leg but not before giving her ankle a kiss and placing it back into my lap.

"The entire situation is shitty at best and I don't blame you for what Linley did. It just seemed like you were holding back on information and purposely trying to avoid telling me. It makes me think I don't really know you when things are thrown in my face and everyone in the room knows but me."

"You're right and I was withholding things. I feel like ever since I opened the firm, I've had to have my attorney hat on at all times. Always having to be on the defensive about every situation, or knowing certain information but holding back to make sure my client doesn't suffer for it. And I did that with you. I was trying to be in boyfriend and attorney mode at the same time doing damage control, and it wasn't working. You are and will always be my number one priority and I'm sorry if you felt otherwise. I never want to hold back from you and I'll tell you everything you want to know. No secrets."

"I would appreciate that," she says nodding.

"Also, my grandparents have been blowing up my phone; they wanted to see you before they left for their Montana home for the next few months. When they found out what happened, they wanted to come see you, but you'd just left with your dad."

"Montana is a very popular state for the retired crew because Saylor's grandparents headed up there last week after stopping by and seeing me," I mention. "I'd love to go see your grandparents. Do you think Grandma would make me her strawberry cheese-cake?" Everly has a very special place in their hearts. They are always asking when I'm going to pop the question so that I can start my little family.

"She'd make you one for every day of the month if it meant you came to see her," I say honestly.

We settle back down on the couch, "Thank you for all the packages you sent. I felt bad for the poor delivery kid, Steven, until he mentioned what you were paying him," she says with a giggle. I paid the kid three hundred dollars a week to make sure she got her daily package at the same time every day. "You didn't need to send me something every day but I loved them."

"Yes I did. I wanted to make sure you had something to look forward to and try to keep your spirits up."

"Having someone other than my dad help me bathe, was pretty nice. Thank you for doing that. It was great to start my day feeling clean and pampered." She leans forward and presses her lips to mine. I let her take the lead and when she pulls away, I fist my hands from reaching out to keep her plastered to me. "How did you know what to send me? And how did you get some of the items personalized so quickly?"

Moment of truth.

"Your dad helped," I admit.

"My dad?" She sounds shocked and I can't blame her because I was too.

"He reached out to me two days after you went home," I say and she looks surprised. "I was shocked too, believe me. He told me you were settled in and we had a long talk over the phone. I flew in the next day and stayed at the motel in town. We met briefly because he needed to get back to you and needed to grab you a few things. I knew then that I wanted to send you something so I asked him if it would be okay. He agreed as long as it didn't upset you. I went home the next day but then found myself flying in every Friday and leaving late Sunday evenings."

"But you never came by the house."

"You asked for space and I wanted to give you that."

"You came all that way and stayed in the motel?"

"Being in the same town you were in was enough. Your dad and I texted almost every day so it was enough then."

"That's just crazy."

"I'd do it again if it meant you were happy and healing. My

biggest restraint was when you started hiking. I was a nervous wreck waiting to hear from Tommy. I was so worried you would fall or get hurt."

"I love hiking in the forest."

"I know, your dad sent me some pictures and you looked so happy out there."

"I do miss being out in the woods. Saylor and I grew up getting lost and finding our way back home."

"Maybe you could take me some time?" I ask.

"I'd love that."

A knock on the door interrupts us.

"Must be dinner, stay put," I tell her and hop up from the couch. Before I leave the living room to answer the door, I turn back around and face her. She's watching me with a questioning look. "Go out with me tomorrow," I say. "On a date."

"Okay?" She sounds so unsure and I must seem crazy to her right now. "Why did you ask it like that?"

"I feel like we need a fresh start and this is it."

"Does that mean we have to wait for a certain period of time before we can move to the next base?"

That makes me laugh.

"If you want but I want you to know that I'm in this all the way till the end."

"I would hope so if you're telling me that you love me," she says with a raised eyebrow.

"You know I do."

There's another knock on the door and this time it's louder. I give her a wink then turn on my heels.

Yup, I'm putting a ring on her finger by the end of summer.

CHAPTER EIGHTEEN

"Are you almost ready?" I hear Linc call out from the living room.

It's been a month since I came home from staying with Dad and Linc and I have seen each other almost every day since. Dad stayed a few days to make sure I was settled in but left after the three of us went to dinner. Linc and Dad got along well and it was nice to see that since I know things got pretty heated when I was in the hospital.

"Mr. Bryant, it's nice to see you again," Linc stood from the table and reached out his hand for Dad to shake.

"Call me Tommy," Dad told him as they shook.

The evening was great and they both discussed his military career as Linc opened up about what happened to his parents and little sister when he was young. We talked about visiting Dad for a few weeks at the end of summer and he was thrilled that Linc was wanting to go fishing out on the lake.

Something else that both Dad and Linc bonded over was my new security man, Sonny. The man is as big as a house but is quick like a puma. Linc made sure to include Dad on the interviews and selection, which I'm sure added more brownie points in his favor.

"Five more minutes," I yell out as I curl the last few locks of hair.

The reflection in the mirror doesn't look like the woman I was two months ago. I'm not beaten or bruised. I've got my glow back and I look just as happy as I was. I still have some aches with my arm but physical therapy is pushing me to be stronger every day.

"You are so gorgeous," I hear and see Linc come into the bathroom of his place.

"Thank you," I reply. "You don't look half bad yourself."

I finish the last curl, and grab for the spray to keep them all in place and then unplug the curling iron I have stored here. I spritz a light layer of perfume, across my body before following Linc out of the bedroom and into the living room. I notice a set of balloons on the counter with an envelope.

"Come here for a sec," Linc tells me from across the room.

I walk over as I start to hear soft music playing in the background.

"What's going on?" I ask, then try to wrack my brain thinking I've forgotten an important date or birthday.

"I know that you aren't ready for me to get on one knee yet but I was hoping we could maybe take this next step together and see where it'll lead us." He picks up the envelope and hands it to me.

Over the last month, Linc has made sure that I receive a special gift each week. It's either delivered to me at work, my apartment, or here at his place. Throughout the day, he'll take time to send me texts, letting me know he is thinking of me.

I hold the gift in my hand very delicately. Each gift is so special and you can tell a lot of thought is put into each one. I turn it over and slide my finger under the flap, opening it up. Inside is a keycard and a physical key. I turn them both over thinking that there is something written on them. When I find nothing, I look back up at Linc.

"These are the keys to the penthouse and garage," he says.

"Okay, thank you Linc," I tell him. He tried to give them to me before I was attacked but I told him it was too soon to be sharing something like that.

"I want you to use them every day and not have our doorman letting you in." He moves in closer and circles his arms around my waist, drawing me in close to his body. I place my hands up on his chest. "I want you to move in with me."

I gasp, "Linc."

"I know we wanted to take things slow this round but I hate when you or I leave for the evening, to go back to an empty place. I want you with me all the time. I want to come home and see your naked body laid out on the couch. Or shower together every morning before we go into work. I just want you here."

I look up into his blue eyes and smile.

"I want that too," I say and watch as his eyes widen in shock. I can tell he was expecting me to put up a fight and that he'd try and negotiate a timeframe.

"Really?" he asks, making sure he heard me correctly.

"Really," I say.

He leans down and captures my lips to his. His tongue caresses the seam of my lips and I open as he swipes his tongue against mine. Using his hands, he pulls me snug, and then even closer with his hands at my back. Only when we're breathless does he pull back.

"Thought I was gonna have to pull the big guns out to persuade you to live with me. I've been practicing all day," he snorts with a smile.

"And what would you have used if I said no?" I ask.

"Let me show you," he says, then he carefully lifts me beneath my underarms and sets me down on the kitchen island.

His hips nudge open my knees and he slides into the space. Planting both hands on either side of my body, bracketing me into his towering stature, he leans down as I stare up at him. He presses his mouth to my temple then traces down to my jaw. Linc makes sure to nibble on my ear as his hands move to pop the single button at my breast. His fingers glide my straps off my shoulders, as he exposes my naked chest.

"Beautiful," he says when he briefly pulls away from my neck.

He takes one hand then tweaks a nipple as his expert mouth takes in the breast. He starts to suckle, causing my head to fall back in a moment of need.

"How's my argument going so far?" he asks as he switches breasts.

A moan leaves my mouth, instead of words, as I push his face closer with my hand on the back of his head. I feel his chuckle as it vibrates right down to my core, sending tingles throughout my body. His fingers start to push my dress up my thighs, exposing my thong. He yanks the string causing the string to snap against my skin then tosses it behind him.

Linc grabs underneath my knees and hauls me to the edge of the counter, making me jump to balance myself to not fall backwards. In a flash, Linc is on his knees with his head between my legs and his mouth latched to my heat. His tongue lashes at my clit and I yell out at how good it feels. He's got me so worked up that I feel like I may come in the next few seconds.

"That's it, angel. Give me your sweet juices," he coaxes as he plunges a finger into my channel and rubs me in my favorite spot.

"Mmm, babe," I groan as my hips lift up to get closer.

Linc adds another finger, scissoring to open me more as I feel heat flush through my body.

"I'm close," I breathlessly state as he doubles his efforts sucking and licking me. His fingers pick up their momentum.

"Shatter for me, angel," Linc's deep voice sets me off and I splinter apart. My body jolts as the orgasm rips through me.

Before my body floats back down from this euphoric feeling, Linc is up and the sound of his belt can be heard. He makes quick work, unbuttoning his pants and pushing down his boxers in a split second, before he's pulling me further off the counter and impaling me on his hard dick. He doesn't skip a beat as he pumps into me, building me back up for another release I'm not sure I'll survive.

"You feel so good," Linc states as his thrust comes in deep and hard. "You're everything I've ever wanted. Everything that is good." His hips drive into me and I feel my legs start to shake as he holds me into place. "I love you, Everly."

My eyes finally focus on him and I look right into his. "I love you too, Linc."

He leans over and takes my lips in his as he devours me. One of his thumbs starts to strum my little ball of nerves at my core and I explode again into a million pieces. Linc pumps three more times before I feel his warm cum coating my walls, and goes slack.

I'm laid back on the cold countertop, with him draped over me catching our breath, when a chime sounds on his phone. He finally lifts his head up off my naked breasts and looks up at me.

"That's the alarm for us to head to the restaurant," he tells me.

"I thought we were supposed to leave earlier?"

"I wanted to make sure we had enough time to celebrate."

"Wait! How did you know that I'd say yes?" I question.

"I told you that my negotiation skills are life changing," he boasts and it makes me laugh. "I love you Everly and one day soon you'll be saying yes to taking my last name too."

"Let's enjoy this celebration first before we jump too far ahead," I say but in the back of my mind, I already know what I'd say when he does ask.

"Let's get cleaned up then head out to meet your friend and her man," he says as he stands up and slowly disengages us. "Mmhmm, feels good every time."

"We better go before you change your mind and we stay here all night," I tell him as he helps me down from the island.

"We could always reschedule."

"No way, I've been wanting you to meet Saylor for a while now. Plus, she's got something important to tell me."

"Okay, but we're leaving and having dessert here at our place in our bed."

"I agree to your terms counselor," I say and he swats me on my butt before I can clear the living room.

"That's why I get paid the big bucks, angel."

Linc and I are sitting down at the table at a small restaurant, near the Santa Monica Pier. Saylor and I love a good Tex-Mex place so Linc thought we'd love this one. I read a text from Saylor, then look up to Linc.

"They're about to walk in," I tell him as he checks his phone. "Everything okay?"

"Yeah, I need to stop in on Levi after this. I told him to take some time off and he hasn't been checking in as much as I wanted," He tells me. "Plus, it'll be good to introduce the two of you."

"I'd love to meet your brother."

I look up and watch as Saylor comes in and heads right for our table. She has the biggest smile on her face and if it were possible, she seems to float over our way. I'm excited to see who the man is that has brought such joy and happiness to my best friend.

I get up and we embrace. We haven't seen each other much over the last month since I spend most of my time at Linc's place, or doing something with him after work.

"You look so good," I tell her, holding both of her hands.

"Thanks, so do you. Let's promise never to go that long again without seeing each other."

"I promise," I agree and look behind her for her man. "Are you here alone?"

"No, he had to step into the restroom for a sec. He'll be here soon."

"Okay, well, Saylor, this is Lincoln Thorne. Linc this is my best friend Saylor," I introduce.

"Nice to meet you, Saylor. Everly has told me so much about you," he greets her, shaking her hand.

"Did you say Thorne?" Saylor looks back over at me confused.

"Yeah, why?"

"It's just that—"

"Sorry, had to—" the man that I saw at the hospital comes over to our table as we're standing there meeting each other.

"What the hell?" Linc says in surprise.

I turn to see what my boyfriend is commenting on but he's looking right at Saylor's boyfriend.

"Do y'all know Levi?" Saylor asks.

"Do I know him?" Linc questions her like it's the most absurd thing he's ever heard. "Levi is my baby brother."

"Wait, wait, wait," I say, trying to help connect some dots here. "Did you know that Levi and Linc were related?" I ask Saylor.

"No but when you said Thorne I thought it was a weird co-incidence for a split second." She turns to Levi. "Did you know that Everly and I were best friends?"

Levi blushes at slightly being called out. "I only found out after she was in the hospital. I was helping Olivia on some of the cases when I saw the photos of her injuries. I put two and two together."

"And you didn't think that was something you thought you should share with me?" Saylor places both hands on her hips, ready for battle.

"I thought we'd meet much sooner but then she left the city and I didn't want what she and Linc were going through to affect us or our relationship."

"That's a fair point but we will be talking about this later," she tells him and he leans down and nuzzles her neck whispering something to her. She lets out a giggle and I feel like we are intruding on a private moment.

"Can we sit and not be subjected to my little brother groping his girl in public," Linc says, breaking the two love birds up.

We all take our seats as the waiter comes over to take our drink and food orders. After he leaves, Saylor and I both start launching in, questioning the other's partner on some details.

"So where did you two meet?" I ask as I scoop up some salsa on a chip.

"We actually met that first night at the bar when you and Lincoln went across the street for coffee. I was at the bar ordering more beer for the table and he was talking to some guy about renovating a kitchen," Saylor jumps in and tells us, with stars in her eyes. She seems so dazzled by Levi that I'm starting to think aliens might have abducted her body.

"Really? The same night?"

"Yep."

Our food comes and our server asks if we need anything else and I look over at my best friend.

"Do you want to split the watermelon or strawberry margarita?"

Anytime we eat Mexican food we always share our drinks.

"Oh, umm, not tonight. I'm not drinking," she says and doesn't sound like herself but then looks over at Levi. I raise my eyebrows when she looks back over at me, letting her know that I know something is going on.

"What was the news you wanted to tell me in person?" I ask when we finally start to dig into our meal. Linc and Levi have been talking about the firm and their other brother Reid, so I focus on Saylor and what she's hiding.

Her eyes soften even more and I watch as she reaches over for Levi's hand, ending their conversation.

"I really want you to support this decision. And you're the first to know." She starts.

"Wait, are you okay?" I ask, my stomach starts to do flips at the anticipation.

"Yes, I'm fine," she says. "Levi and I got married a couple of months ago—"

"What the fuck?" Linc interrupts. "Is that true?" he sounds more hurt than accusatory.

"We love each other and didn't want to wait," Levi tries to justify to his big brother and I can see the redness creeping up his neck. I'm staring like Levi is a big marshmallow. He definitely is a pushover and people pleaser.

"You got married and didn't think that I'd want to be there to cheer you on or support you on the biggest day of your life?" I ask Saylor. I feel a pang of sadness in my chest, not being included in this with her. Growing up we fantasied about what our weddings would be like and how we would be with each other every step of the way.

"But to get married without me there? Do Mom and Dad know? What about Reid? When I told you to go out and take some time off to find yourself, this wasn't what I was talking about." Linc chimes in before Saylor can answer me.

"We wanted it to just be us, then we'd have a big reception at a later date." Levi tries to explain. "Please don't be mad at me." I can hear the distress in his voice from across the table and watch as Saylor reaches over to comfort him.

Linc reaches over the table and yanks Levi up to where they are standing. He pulls him into a big hug and tells him something only the two of them can hear. I turn to give them their privacy and focus my attention on my fiery best friend.

"What am I chop liver? Why didn't you tell me?"

"You had just gotten hurt, then left. You had so much on your plate and a long road to recovery. I didn't want to add to it at the moment. I love you so much and you were hurting so bad when you left with your dad."

"I know," I tell her and I know she's right. I wasn't in the right headspace for that kind of news. "Please tell me from now on no matter what is going on, okay?"

"Okay!"

Linc and Levi sit back down and Levi puts an arm around Saylor and brings her close, kissing her temple. As Linc places a hand on my bare thigh, giving it a squeeze, I turn my head to his and he gives me a reassuring kiss.

"Well, we have some news too, that just happened?"

"Really?"

"Linc and I are moving in together," I announce.

"Ohmygosh, that's so exciting!" Saylor says.

"We think so," Linc beams as he takes a drink of his beer.

"I'm happy for you Lincoln. I feel like we're where we are supposed to be in life for the first time," Levi says and Linc gives him a nod.

We are at the end of the meal and I watch as Saylor yawns.

"You're tired, so early?" I ask. This is the time we are usually ready to go out.

"Yeah, I can't hang like I used to," she says then looks over at Levi giving him a *look.*

"Go ahead if you want," he tells her.

She looks back over at me, biting her bottom lip.

"I have some other news."

"Okay?" my heart drops thinking she's got a medical condition she just found out about.

"You've got to be kidding me, Levi," Linc says under his breath but I can't look over at him because I'm so focused on what she is about to say.

"I'm pregnant," she says and I think I lose the ability to hear sounds. My ears hear a white noise and I watch her mouth moving, but I can't hear what she's saying. I'm in shock.

"What do you mean you're pregnant? How?" I ask. "I mean I know how babies are conceived but you just got married."

"We were shocked too and it's still very early on so we don't know anything yet. I just took the test this morning and all three came back positive."

"Are you happy?"

"I'm so happy," she admits.

I get up from my seat and she does the same. We hug and cry for what seems like hours but only minutes. Of all people, Saylor is the one person in this world that deserves true happiness in her life.

"Then I'm so happy for you. And Levi. And my niece or nephew," I tell her with tears in my eyes.

"Thank you, Everly."

"I love you Saylor and nothing will ever change that," I tell her.

"Love you too."

"I think this calls for a celebration," Linc calls out and whistles for someone. Just then, a mariachi band comes over and starts to serenade our table, as both of our men come up to us and start to slow dance as the music plays.

"You alright, angel?" Linc asks as we sway.

"I've never been better."

EPILOGUE

3 MONTHS LATER

"Do you know which courtroom you'll be in today?" I ask from the bathroom as I finish getting ready.

"Not sure. I'll have to check the email Olivia sent," Linc says back from the bedroom.

"Well, text it to me and I'll stop in after I finish paying for my ticket."

Once again I have to go down to the courthouse and pay for a parking ticket. I'd been doing so well and it'd been months since my last one. I still don't even know why I got this one. I checked before I even got out of the car to make sure that I was in the correct zone.

"Do you want to ride together to the courthouse?" Linc asks from the doorframe.

"No, because you might be there all day and I've got one of my last physical therapy sessions."

"Maybe if court ends early, we can grab some lunch before your session?" He offers.

"I'd love that."

My recovery is going great and I've almost built all my muscle strength back up. At the spa, I work more on the management side of things, and only do thirty-minute massages or less right now if I'm needed to fill in for someone.

Linley Lewis took a plea deal after finding out that she wasn't going to be able to cop with the insanity case. She agreed to serve twelve years with possibility for parole in nine. Olivia, who apparently knows everyone or has connections in every corner of this world, worked very hard to make sure she was given the strictest punishment she could get for all six charges that were brought up against her. She said that she called in a lot of markers to make this happen. The tabloids ate her up and spit her out in the media. It was definitely not the press she was hoping for. Olivia is wanting to sue her in civil court and for the damages done to me. Her attorney has already made a deal with us and I gave every cent to SafePlace, Linc's foundation. That money is going to help build another building since the one he has is now at capacity.

"I'll see you later, angel," Linc comes over and kisses my forehead. "I'll text you the courtroom number."

He doesn't wait for me to kiss him back before he's gone. Linc's been really stressed the last week. I'm sure it has to do with his case he has today. He usually doesn't get worried but for some reason this case is putting him through his paces.

I finish up in the bathroom, then head out to the garage to my car. Linc said after this ticket he's getting me my own version of Dale, his security guy/driver, but I'm holding firm for as long as I can. I really only go to a few places because most of the time I'm at home, work, or at Saylor and Levi's place. She's four and a half months pregnant and barely looks like she's carrying a baby. She really only looks bloated after eating too much at lunch.

I park in the designated parking space for the courthouse and start to walk up the steps to the doors. As I enter, I can't help but remember the last time I was here and it puts a smile on my face. If it wasn't for a parking ticket, I might never have met Linc.

As I reach the steps that lead up to the second floor, I check the ticket to make sure I still need to go to room 208 like last time.

"Do you need some help, angel?" I hear a familiar voice ask.

I look up from my ticket and see the absolute perfect blue eyes staring down at me. He touches my upper arm when I don't respond fast enough and I feel a jolt like I always do when we touch.

"I'm heading upstairs to pay a parking ticket," I tell him.

"I can walk you over there and show you, if you want," he offers, then sweeps his hand toward the stairs that lead up to the next floor.

It's like Deja Vu all over again and I play along as we ascend the stairs.

"Do you work here?" I ask as I check him out.

The moment we get to the top of the stairs, my eyes widen as I see rose petals down the hall, that stop right in front of room 208. Linc takes a hold of my hand and leads me to the end of the path. My hands are shaking and my knees wobble as he gets down on one knee.

"I never knew what living was until I met you all those months ago, here at the courthouse. I will forever be grateful for you breaking the law and having to come here," he says and I laugh. "There's not an image of my future that doesn't have you in it. My world begins and ends with you, angel. Please do me the greatest pleasure of all and marry me. Marry me and be with me until we are old and grey. Be with me through the good and bad times. Through all of our future children's and grandchildren's lives. I love you so much, Everly. Will you marry me?"

He reaches into his pocket pulling out a jewelry box and opens it. I don't even have to look at it before I'm telling him my answer.

"Yes! Yes, Linc, I will marry you," I sob as I throw my arms around him and kiss him with everything I have in me.

I hear clapping and cheers echoing down the hall, making us break our celebration. Our friends and family are all surrounding us with cameras. Once Linc slides the ring on my finger, everyone converges on us with love and hugs. After we take a million pictures, the crowd starts to thin out.

"Are you happy future Mrs. Thorne?" Linc asks, pulling me in for another hug and kiss.

"So happy, future husband," I respond and then call out to our family, "Does anyone know where the Justice of the Peace is located?"

"Room 323," Levi yells out and we all laugh knowingly. I do catch the disapproving look from Daniel, Linc and Levi's dad. Linc had mentioned that he wasn't happy with them getting married so fast. But anyone who knows Levi and Saylor know that they love each other so much. In two weeks, they plan to tell the family that they are pregnant. We're hosting everyone at our penthouse for the big reveal.

"Love you, angel."

"Love you too."

Linc
FOUR DAYS LATER

"Mr. Lincoln, Levi is here to see you," Ruby announces over the phone's intercom. There's a muffled sound, then she starts to whisper, "He doesn't look well."

"Send him in," I respond, thinking how odd her remark is.

Within seconds, the door opens and a disheveled Levi comes into the office and straight over to the windows. He's in a pair of jeans and a graphic shirt. He looks like he hasn't slept in days and it worries me.

"Is everything okay bub?" I ask, needing to know if I should call anyone.

"No," he says in a defeated tone and it has my back sitting ramrod straight, bracing myself for this conversation.

"What's going on?" I go to stand but stay right next to the chair. I'm not trying to overwhelm him until I hear everything he needs to get out.

"I," he pauses for a moment before he turns around to face me. "I need your help on two things."

"Anything. You name it and I'll make it happen," I tell him because I would help hide a body without hesitation. Besides Everly, he is the only other person I'd cross lines for.

He starts to run his hands over his face, then through his messy hair.

"There is someone trying to kill Saylor and I need to find out who it is," he says and I can hear the desperation in his voice.

My knees bend and I fall down into the chair. A lot of thoughts start to swirl around my head trying to figure out if I heard him correctly, or if this is something that's been blown out of proportion.

"What do you mean someone is trying to kill Saylor?" I speak slowly and evenly to make sure I'm understanding all of this.

"For the last month, someone has been making threats and yesterday they almost made good on them."

"We need to go to the police, Levi," I start to say, as I type into my contacts.

"No police."

"And what was the second thing you needed help with?" I place both hands on the desk, wanting to know if it's about to get worse.

"I want a divorce—"

WANT TO KNOW WHAT HAPPENS TO
LEVI AND SAYLOR?
Their story is coming this FALL!

THANK YOU so much for reading *Linc*!
I hope you loved it and will leave a review.

This series was a labor of love and I enjoyed writing Linc and Everly so much. It was a huge change writing this series compared to my mafia one but I love it all the same. These brothers are completely different, other than loving their women, and I can't wait for you to experience them.

I'd love to hear from you so let's get social!
Join my newsletter for sneak peeks and
special project opportunities:

Follow me along this journey for updates on
the current and next projects.

www.AmberAllee.com

Goodreads:
www.goodreads.com/author/show/48624101.Amber_Allee

Facebook Page:
www.facebook.com/AmberAlleeAuthor

Facebook Group:
www.facebook.com/groups/655580198616583

Instagram:
www.instagram.com/author.amberallee

TikTo:
www.tiktok.com/@author.amberallee k

ALSO BY AMBER ALLEE

Las Vegas Mafia Series
THE PRINCE
HIDDEN QUEEN
BISHOP

Thorne Brother Series
LINC
LEVI

ACKNOWLEDGMENTS

Kevin, Kevin, Kevin: the love of my life, thorn in my side, and whom is the only person who understands and puts up with me on the daily. I love you more every day and your support through this journey has truly shown me just how much you love me. Thank you for supporting my dream and all the other crazy adventures I get us into.

Mom and Dad, thank you for always supporting me and showing up. I'll never be more thankful because being your daughter has been the best blessing. We do everything together as a family and I wouldn't change all the memories we have made and that my kids get to experience with you as we get older.

Becky, my MIL, thank you for being my biggest cheerleader on every book and every launch.

Misti K, you are the best PA/friend/organizer/anything & everything around! Thank you for doing everything so that I could write this book. I'd be lost twiddling my thumbs if it wasn't for you! You make life so easy and you truly are amazing. Love ya!

Stacey B, as always you make the insides look BEAUTIFUL! Thank you for working with me in creating the perfect book.

Stacy G, thank you for creating this gorgeous cover. I love how you are able to find and create a sexy work of art! They always look perfect and exactly what I envisioned.

Andrea B, thank you for being amazing and working so hard on edits with me. Thank you for being patient and working so quickly to get this done.

M.E. Carter, thank you for making sure the story was smooth and flowed! Thank you for working me in and all your helpful tips and advice.

To the Readers, thank you so much for continuing to support me through this journey. Your reviews and kind messages fuel me to be a better writer. I always love hearing your thoughts on all the characters.

To the Promoters & Influencers, thank you for getting my book out there and seen by the readers. You guys make such a difference for indie authors like me and I am so thankful for each and every one of you.

Kristen Portillo, you'll never see this because you were taken from us way too soon, but I want you to know that I'm such a better person simply by having known you. You had been my rock since my very first manuscript and I'm not sure how to navigate through all this without your emails and words that help me along the way. Please know that I think of you often and am heartbroken for your family and the book community. Thank you for taking a chance on a nobody and giving me the strength to become a better writer with each book. Love ya girl!

ABOUT THE AUTHOR

Amber Allee is a new author with her debut novel, *The Prince*, released in early 2024. She has since completed the Las Vegas Mafia Series and it is available now. Her next series, *The Thorne Brothers*, is expected to come out in June of 2025. She started writing in 2015, but finally pulled the trigger to publish recently. Amber loves to write about romance, drama, and suspense featuring hot alpha heroes.

She lives in the great state of Texas, in the same town she grew up in. She lives there with her husband and two kids. When she isn't writing, Amber can be found under blankets reading or playing games with her family. She loves to travel and shop. She is a lover of wearing animal print and everything that sparkles!